Wraith Consumed

Demon Cursed Book 4

Charmaine Ross

Excerpt

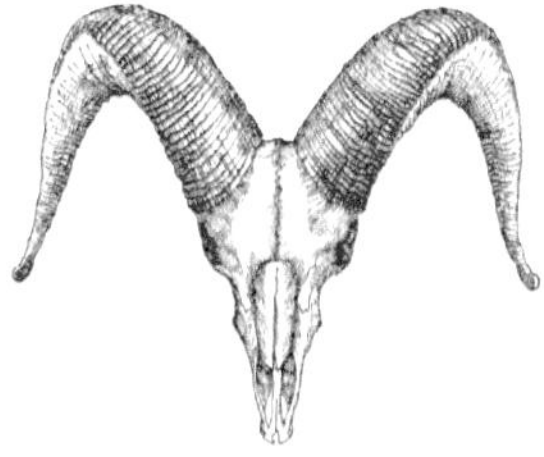

"I don't think you understand the length I'll go to, to protect you." Elliot's voice was low. A solemn vow made to me. My fingers sunk into his hair as I gazed at him. The weight of his words wrapped around me. They were the same words I say back to him in a heartbeat. There was nothing I wouldn't do for him. He was mine. He was *everything*.

He leaned down to kiss me, his lips crashing against mine. He slid his tongue inside my mouth, catching my doubts with each deep sweep. I moaned into his mouth, needing every bit of himself that he'd give me. He drugged me with his lips and tongue, and melted my body with each caress and squeeze of his hands.

I wanted more than just this time; much more than this once that could be our last time together.

Elliot drew his pants off, and then he was between my parted thighs. His hard, hot length slid through my folds in the most exquisite way. I was wet, ready and waiting for him. I ground myself against him, clit throbbing, groaning when a frisson of sparks rushed through me as he settled his weight over my lower body.

"Please, Elliot. Please." My mouth watered as he tilted his hips, gliding through my wetness. I was so sensitive that I cried out, my nerves on fire. My desire to have him inside me built to overflowing.

"You never have to wait for me," Elliot groaned.

I burned from the inside out as he notched the tip of himself to my entrance then slid inside my willing body, locking my gaze with his until he'd seated every glorious inch of himself inside me to the hilt. So full. So complete. My back arched, and I cried out at his welcome invasion, fingers clawing his arms, mouth falling open on a breathless moan.

His fingers tangled in my hair as he titled my head back and kissed me. My hands shook as I buried them in his hair, wrapping him in my arms around his neck, his shoulders, his waist. I opened my legs, cradling him between my thighs. He crushed his pelvis against mine, putting pressure on my clit. The muscles in my channel squeezed him, searing me with heat. He throbbed inside me, his shaft pulsing, and we both groaned.

He dragged himself out of me before slamming back. His pelvis rubbed my clit, liquefying my body, each thrust exquisite torture. He filled me thoroughly. Deeply. Giving his whole self to me, completing me in a way that no one else ever could. The sounds of his gravelly moans filled my ears. Every thrust hit the deepest part of me. His pelvis hit mine, rubbing and pounding against the most intimate parts of my body. I tilted my hips, accepting each thrust, wanting more. Always wanting more.

His body covered mine, from hips to shoulders. He kissed me, thrusting into my mouth with his tongue the way he thrust into my core. His perspiration mingled with mine; his body locked with mine. Two halves coming together as a whole.

My eyelids closed, white power washing the darkness away. Impressions of faces formed from within the power. Faces I felt I should know but couldn't define. They spun around me, teasing me with meaning just out of my reach. Metaphorical hands extended towards me and as I strained for them licking flames of power cut me off from them. My climax broke through me, hurtling me away from the power and the faces as exquisite pleasure exploded through me.

Elliot pulsed inside me. His body tensed, his fingers firmed in my hair, and his moan washed around me, mixing with my pleasure-filled scream as I shattered into a thousand pieces. I spiralled with my climax to that place where we met on a soul level. His energy brushed against mine, welcome, calming.

I floated back, sated. Elliot rolled me to my side, still inside me, holding me tenderly, kissing me, petting me, looking at me as though committing me to memory. As though he didn't believe that we would win.

As though this was the last time we would make love and this was the last time he'd hold me in his arms.

Blurb

The angelic power given to me is fracturing me apart. I've crossed the veil, but I don't know who I am or how I can to be here.

Ibn, the professor on the University of Creation, shows me my Akashic records to help me remember my past lives, but it doesn't work. Demons attack. I ward them off using my power, calling a man so achingly familiar to me through a portal I created.

Elliot knows me. He tells me I am his soul-mate. I want to believe him but the power inside me is unstable. Angelic power was never meant to be contained by a human soul. All dimensions of reality will collapse if I can't contain it.

Captured by demons, I must fight Lilith and remember who I really am before I fracture apart completely. Only my fully healed soul stands between Lilith's rule and total annihilation of every plane of existence.

Fans of Laura Thalassa's 'Four Horsemen', I.T. Lucas 'Children of the Gods', and K. F. Breene 'Demigods' will devour this paranormal romance filled with angels, demons and impossible odds.

Wraith Consumed is the fourth in the Demon Cursed series. If you like strong heroines that fight for the truth, lost souls that sacrifice all and the answer to the afterlife itself, dive into this exciting series today!

Contents

Chapter One

Time stretched into infinity, a never-ending sea of white, comfort and contentment. I closed my eyes, sighing into the serenity and drifting in the peace. I floated in warmth, hung in a cocoon of semi-consciousness where nothing mattered. I neither worried about where I was nor concerned myself beyond the moment in which I existed.

Voices punched through my tranquillity, insistent and urgent. They didn't belong here. I didn't want to hear them. I was happy here, in this place of non-existence. I wanted to stay where it was quiet. Where I could just be. Where nothing and nobody wanted me. Where nothing and nobody compelled me to do anything except drift.

That's all I wanted to do, except something niggled at the edge of my consciousness. A stubborn tickle that wouldn't go away. I focussed on it and as I did, the concept of worry slid away, leaving me to float in the vast white sea of comfort and safety.

The voices followed, a trumpet of harsh sounds that had no place disturbing me. They grew disruptive enough for me to distinguish two of them, their urgent arguing drawing unwanted attention. As I was sucked towards them, blurred edges cleared and sound became recognisable.

"She's not coming round, Keira," the voice, male, said. The edge of worry made me drift closer, curious.

"That's highly unusual. It's been days since she came here," a soft female voice, I assumed Keira, said. "She's not anchoring."

"That's because she's not from either dimension," the male said. "She's retained her physical body as well as her soul, and both are fighting for survival."

"How can that even happen?" Keira whispered and in my semi-conscious state I heard her disbelief.

"It should be impossible, but here she is," the male said, sharing her tone.

A long moment passed. Enough for me to drift away, content to forget their bafflement. Even though I was the subject, there was no desire to understand any more. I just wanted to cocoon myself and let myself flow wherever the white would take me.

"If she doesn't anchor, Ibn, her soul will disintegrate," Keira said.

At least I had a name for both the male and female now, Ibn and Keira. They weren't familiar to me. At least I didn't think they were.

A flicker of worry brushed against a faraway corner inside my head. A shadow of a thought flickered. Unsustainable. An urge pressed down on me. There was something I had to do, something important. It niggled, then slid away, taking with it any momentary worry that might have come with the thought.

It was no longer important. The white blankness called me, tempting me to drift away from the voices. I could close my eyes and rest and just *be*.

"It's not only her soul that is in jeopardy. The power running through her is fracturing her," Ibn said. My forehead tingled with the brush of cool fingertips. I jerked at the physical touch, unused to feeling anything.

"She moved!" Keira said.

"The band, Keira," Ibn said. I wanted to drift away, to sink into the warm comfort. The whiteness beckoned, tempting me with its nothingness, but those fingertips never left my forehead, locking me in the physical.

I tried to brush them away and sank into a heaviness that had no right intruding in my languid state. I grew heavy as I settled into my body. The pure white light grew darker, spotting with shadows that formed the silhouette of two faces hovering above me.

Their blurred shapes cleared enough for me to see furrowed brows and concern in their eyes. Keira's blue eyes grew wide, her mouth opening with a small, sharp inhale as she looked down at me.

"Quickly, Keira. Bring it to me," Ibn said. Sleek brows lowered across eyes so brown they were nearly black, set over a prominent nose and full lips. Something about the eyes made me pause to focus on them. Ibn was a young man, maybe in his early thirties, but those eyes held the knowledge of lifetimes. They were also filled with worry as they peered at me.

Those weren't the eyes that I wanted on me, though. These eyes were wrong. The wrong shape, wrong colour. Emerald eyes flashed at the forefront of my mind. Eyes that looked at me in a way that made me want to bask in their warmth. Familiar eyes. Eyes that caused a bittersweet blade to slide through my heart.

They were important in a way that made the breath stick in my lungs, that propelled me with the urge to go somewhere. Do something. The urgent niggle started at the back of my head and exploded through my mind, shattering into shards of glass.

Light flashed off gold, dazzling me as Keira handed Ibn a thin, u-shaped band. He set the band over my forehead. Cold iced through my head, scattering the splinters as though they'd never existed, leaving me with an endless black vacuum inside my skull. The band tightened, lacing across my forehead and around my skull. A blinding flash of heat slashed through the frost in my brain, leaving me gasping for air as though there wasn't any oxygen left in my lungs.

My vision wavered through tears as my mind and soul continued to fracture. The frantic voices of Keira and Ibn were white-noise behind the roar inside my head. My body flashed hot and cold as violent tremors shook my bones. My back arched, the back of my head drove into the soft surface beneath me and my body bowed around the agony ripping through me.

Fragmented images spun through my mind. Visions of faces so beautiful they were spun from light, familiar faces that held me in the arms of belonging, things 'other' brought forth from my worst nightmare, betrayal coating them all with thick, black tar. The face with the green eyes flashed past my consciousness. I grasped for that face as though my life depended on him. Need. Want. Desperate love compressed into a hard knot of longing strong enough to cleave my heart in two.

That man. I needed him as much as he needed me. As though the cusp of life trembled between us. When I reached for him, he wasn't there, but a stab of pain pierced my eyeballs and obliterated his face, leaving empty darkness.

"Who is Elliot?" Keira's voice floated at the edges of my consciousness.

"I don't know. I can't see any of her connections. They're too disrupted," Ibn's muffled voice replied.

Elliot. The name was familiar, but when I tried to form an image in my mind of who that could be, agony sliced through my brain, obliterating the name as well as my ability to speak.

A gentle hand curved over my forehead and warmth imbued through skin and bone, easing my muscles. I sank back to the mattress, my muscles easing with a sigh. The warmth stilled my mind, and I wallowed in the darkness behind closed lids, swimming in the absence of pain.

"Is she asleep?" Keira asked.

I cracked open eyelids that were too damn heavy. I wanted to tell them to leave me alone so I could be asleep. Twin faces wavered above me. Keira's gaze darted from Ibn to me, or more appropriately, to the centre of my forehead. Her blonde, wavy hair fluffed as she moved away from me. Ibn's shoulders sagged, and his face lost some of the tense lines that had bracketed his eyes and mouth.

Ibn's palm slipped from my forehead, leaving a lingering warmth. My vision cleared, yet the hollow in my head remained. Now I could think a little more clearly, I found myself lying in a comfortable bed, a soft blanket over me to my shoulders.

A warm, gentle breeze ruffled a transparent curtain, the air bringing with it the sweetness of fresh roses. Sunlight diffused into the room, making it light-filled, warm and comfortable. There was something innately safe about this room. The same feeling 'home' brought, if home could be described as a blank slate. The room was nothing more than white walls, undisturbed by paintings or adornments. A white bedside table was next to my head.

Keira poured a glass of water from a tumbler on a white buffet cabinet on the wall adjacent to where I lay and brought it over. I wriggled to my elbows, Ibn helping me to recline on the pillows.

"How are you feeling now?" Ibn asked.

I sipped the water, letting the sweet, cool liquid slide down my throat. I peered at both Keira and Ibn. Ibn's forehead scrunched as he peered over delicate, gold-rimmed glasses perched on his beak-like nose.

"I..." I didn't know how to answer that. The agony that ripped through me had simmered down to a thrumming deep within me. Just a reminder that it hadn't gone away entirely. I looked down at my body tucked under a neat white blanket. "Why is everything white?"

"We find the lack of visual stimulation helps souls adjust," Ibn said.

Breeze wafted through the open window, making the curtains billow. The air was warm without being muggy. It looked to be the perfect day outside. I peered into Ibn's chocolate eyes, his words catching up with me. "Why would souls need to adjust?"

"You've stepped through the veil. Can you recall the name you were known by in your previous life?" Keira asked. She smiled and little lines fanned from the corner of her eyes. She patted the front of the apron she wore over a long skirt that reached the ground. As was the room, her clothing was all white as well.

"I'm..." My name. I tried to remember my name, but the black hole inside my head swallowed anything I reached for. The horrible urgency that pressed down on me from before reared up. "I..."

Ibn put his hand over my fist that clutched the sheets and gave me a reassuring squeeze. His hand was warm. His lips cursed in a smile. "Don't worry. Your memory will come back. We find it can take some time for those souls who suffered at the end."

My forehead tightened as my gaze ran across his clothing. He wore a tan vest over a white tunic that covered his legs and feet. His vest and glasses were the only colour in the room.

"Suffered?" Why was he talking to me about souls and suffering and time? I slipped my hand from beneath his to scrunch the blanket and hold it to my chest. "What are you talking about?"

Ibn shared a quick glance at Keira. "There's nothing to worry about. You just need to rest some more. Then everything will be clear."

He was pacifying me. If he thought that would calm me, he had another thing coming. I wasn't a person who liked to be kept in the dark. I liked to know. To understand. That way, I could work my way through problems. My heart leapt behind the hand at my chest and kept galloping behind my ribs. "You need to tell me what's going on now. I'll worry more if you don't tell me. I don't need to rest."

Adrenaline poured through my limbs, as though I was in the middle of a fight and I'd been punched to the ground. The fight was still going on and I needed to move. I couldn't rest in bed and wait for answers to come. There was no time. I had to...needed to...had to...

I gripped the blanket and pushed it off my legs, throwing them over the edge of the bed. Keira and Ibn reached for me as I went to stand. I shoved their hands away, urgency to get somewhere, to do something strangling me. Only I didn't know where I needed to go or what I had to do. The darkness inside my head erupted, swallowing me whole. I cried out, gripping my head, my palms splayed over the hard metal band about my forehead as pain swallowed me whole.

Ibn placed his palm on mine. White light washed over me, sinking through me until I was surrounded in the warm whiteness where nothing mattered.

Thankfully. Mercifully, I sank to the bottom of the white depths with open arms.

Chapter Two

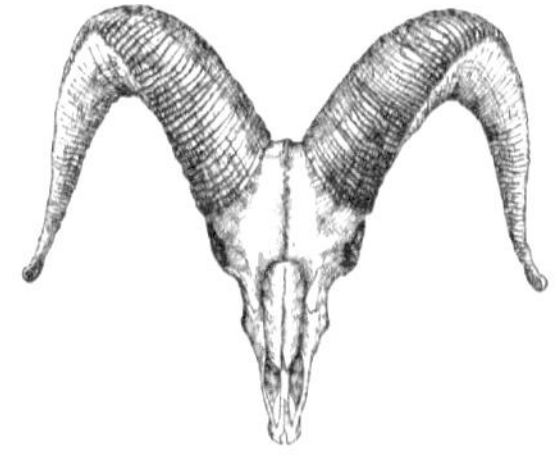

I woke to find myself in a small, quaint bedroom, with wallpapered walls covered in tiny bunches of flowers. A chest of drawers made from gleaming dark wood sat beneath a window. Perched on top was an oval mirror with scalloped edges, a hairbrush, and a wooden jewellery box.

A chair sat in the room's corner with a sun hat on the seat. A matching dark wood wardrobe lined the adjacent wall. A black key was in the lock, holding the doors closed. I sat up slowly, swinging my legs off the mattress.

I was dressed in a light blue gown made of silk. The matching robe pooled on the floor next to the bed and I stepped over to pick it up, throwing it around my shoulders as though I'd done something similar a thousand times before. A pair of beige slippers with a white furred trim were tucked beneath the bed. I slipped them on my feet, finding them a perfect fit.

"Hello?" My voice floated out of the room and echoed into the corridor outside of the room. There didn't seem to be anyone here, wherever here was.

Tying the silk cord about my waist, I stepped from the room to find myself in a short hallway. A carpet runner ran the length of the hall and I followed it past a bathroom fitted with a matching pink bathtub, toilet and basin, and walked into a neat kitchen. Muted creams highlighted leaf green cupboards. A Formica table with four matching chairs was in the centre of the room.

I wandered through the kitchen into a living room. A dark wood mantle framed an open fireplace. I paused, my gaze drifting to the space in front of the fire. My heart kicked as though it remembered something my head didn't.

I ran my fingers across the back of the armchairs. I picked up the top book from a stack on a table next to one chair and ran my fingers over the hand etched illustration of a rather sad face of Nelson Algren's book *'Someone in Boots'.*

I put it back on the stack and moved towards a sunroom that made up the back of the house. A set of windows looked out into a neat little fenced backyard. A small shed sat in one corner. A vegetable patch lined the back wall, filled with cherry tomato plants and bean vines. A tree laden with lemons was nearer the house. On the other side of the window, a heavy-looking rake and shovel leaned against the wall. My fingers twitched as I imagined picking up the shovel and aiming at someone's head.

I jerked, blinking like crazy. Who the hell would pick up a shovel and hit someone with it? An image of my hands wrapped about the handle flew into my mind as my heart pounded in terror. I followed the fragment, needing to know where it led. The tip of memory teased me before sinking into the hole of my mind, desperation licking its heels.

White-hot pain lanced through my head. I fell to my knees, hunched over my thighs and clutched the band around my head.. The darkness in my head yawned open, swallowing me. I clenched my eyes tight, pain lashing through me. I let the shard of memory go in my nerveless head, trembling as the agony subsided.

I panted hard, my chest heaving as my senses settled. I spread my palm on the floorboards, the grains scratchy on my skin, perspiration creating a wet fog around my fingers. Blood pounded in my ears, and my vision wavered before solidifying into clear objects and colours.

I groaned, tipping my head back and sitting up straighter. My head throbbed beneath the hard band. I wrapped my fingers around the warm metal, tugged and succeeded in wrenching my head.

"Ow!" My voice sounded loud in my ears, but it did nothing to loosen the headband.

I yanked the band with both hands now, but it was stuck tight. I felt around my head, searching for a latch or pins, finding nothing. There was no reason for it to be stuck to my head. Why the hell wasn't it coming off?

Skin slick with perspiration, I scrambled onto weak legs and staggered into the bathroom, coming up to the mirror and clutching the basin. I knew the face that started back at me was *me*, but there was nothing familiar about my reflection. I could have been staring at a photo of an actor, or well-known model.

I ran my fingertips across my cheek, down my nose. I couldn't keep my hand from trembling before my attention went to the stone set into the rim of a slim, golden band that sat in the middle of my forehead.

An illegible inscription was etched into the gold. The letters moved as I watched, writing over the metal in ever-changing swirls and curves. I felt them twist under my touch, moving my hand to the end of the band above my ears.

I traced the gem set into the middle of the band, in the dead centre of my forehead. The stone was deep blue, twinkling with glittering spots of white, pink and orange. I leaned closer, watching the gem carefully. It looked as though it contained the universe, as though I could come out the other side of the cosmos if I fell into its rich lustre.

It throbbed with heat; the pulsing sent tingles into my skin that then travelled through my body. I drew in a deep breath, allowing the force it exuded. It helped to centre me. To stave off the terror of the darkness inside my head.

I stumbled away from the basin, turning my back on the familiar, yet not, bathroom and into the hallway. I swayed as lethargy pulled my limbs. My eyes were heavy. My feet lead. I hovered in the doorway of the bedroom, staring at the mussed bed.

Being here made no sense. I didn't understand where I was. Why I was here? An urgency niggled at the edge of my mind, and along with it was the simmering pain ready to swamp me if I tried to dig into the hollow pit behind my eyes.

I found myself at the dressing table, my hand on the wooden jewellery box. I slowly slid the lid off, removing the trinkets. A set of marcasite earrings and matching ring. A sparkle caught my eye as I took out a beautiful, delicate diamond ring. It was an engagement ring. I slid it into my finger, amazed it was a perfect fit.

The niggle started up, an insistent voice in my head that wasn't clear. I knew it was important, but I didn't know why. I spun the ring on my finger, a well of longing and sadness rolling through me. Pressure built behind my eyes and inside my chest. I wiped my cheek as a tear welled and tickled over my lashes.

I took the ring off. Wearing it hurt too much. Happiness, grief and kind emerald eyes washed through me; eyes that followed me, that loved me too much. I winced at the sharp slide of pain behind my eyes and buried the ring under a ruby pendant.

I traced the gem with my fingertip. My mouth dried as I tugged it out. The ruby spun at the end of the chain, catching the light and throwing it around the room as though it burned with an inner light. Fear welled inside me and my fingers were speared with a chill that went bone deep.

I dropped the ruby into the box, stumbling away on numb legs. I had to get out of here. The familiar, yet not, house should be comfortable. I should feel safe here, but I didn't. An element of despair drove through me, shattering the safety I knew should be here.

I didn't know how I knew. I didn't know anything, yet I sensed what I needed to. My vision welled with unshed tears, the room blurring with the bright sunlight filtering through the curtains.

Something about the light. Two faces hovering above me. A woman and a man. The man had put the headband on me. Soul. Suffered. Veil. There was a wrongness to this house. A wrongness in being here. There was something I had to do, and it was urgent. So, so urgent.

I stumbled from the bedroom, my feet taking me to the front door while my head shattered. I twisted the doorknob, but the door didn't budge. I pulled it with all of my strength, but the door remained shut.

My chest tightened, heart pounded, blood rushed. I needed to get out. Out. OUT! Heat welled inside me, racing from somewhere deep in behind my breastbone, shooting through me in a fiery wake of energy. My hands filled with light, glowing from within. Energy poured from my hand into the doorknob, while pain sliced through my head. I didn't care. I held on tight, needing to get the hell away from here. I tugged with everything I had. The door splintered, disintegrated into nothing. The door that had been there was now gone.

Chapter Three

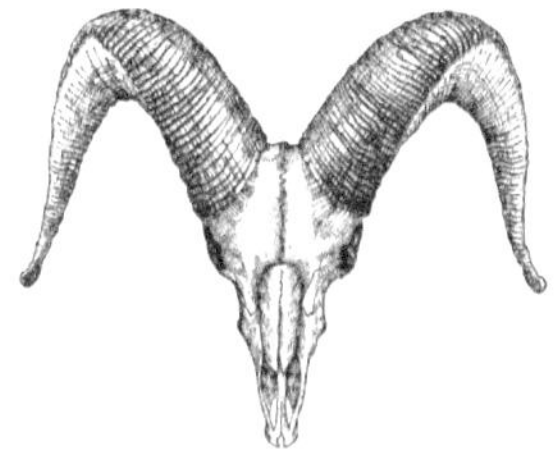

The pillow was smooth and warm beneath my cheek. I pried open my eyes to find myself back in bed. I was getting sick of blacking out and waking up in bed without reason. I sat up, reeling with a wave of dizziness.

"Easy there. No need to rush. We have all the time in the world," a male voice said.

I gasped, turning to his location. The man from the white room sat at the dressing table. He smiled at me, his face lighting up with a warmth that I didn't return. "Who are you?" I said. I was in the same quaint bedroom I'd woken up in before. The room that was vaguely familiar, yet not.

"My name is Professor Ibn al Haytham. It is nice to properly introduce myself to you," he said, pushing his glasses more securely onto his nose.

"Where am I? Why are you here? Why am I here?" I asked and swallowed around a dry throat. No use in beating around the bush. I had questions I needed answered, despite the low-level throbbing in my head.

The professor spoke, unflappable despite the terror riding me. "There's no need to be scared. Far from it, actually. You're here because we thought this would be the most comfortable place for you to wake in, considering the white room caused you undue stress. We manifested it from a fragment in your mind hoping to ease your transition, however I think we may have miscalculated."

I blinked at Professor Ibn. "I don't understand any of that."

"It's true that you display a little more in the way of complications than the norm," Ibn said.

"Complications? The norm?" Nothing he said made a lick of sense. Alarm bells struck like a gigantic claxon in my mind. "How the hell could you manifest this house? You can't manifest a house from my memory? Are you some sort of cult leader? Am I on drugs?"

There was a range of hallucinatory drugs that could bend the mind or create confusion. Doses had to be carefully administered to make sure patients were treated for pain, but not become addicted. *How did I know that?* I winced, bringing my hand to my forehead at the stab of pain. I let the thought pass, and the pain released, focussing on Ibn.

His smile widened, revealing white teeth in his tan face. "That is a very good assumption, but it is not the truth. Tell me, have you recovered any of your memories yet?"

I shook my head. The emptiness inside my skull was inky black. I didn't like being in bed, in a room with someone I didn't know, and sat up, dropping one leg to the floor. "Should I?"

Ibn sighed. "Usually souls don't take so long to recover even from strenuous lives, but you? I can't work out why you came to this dimension. You didn't come through a normal doorway.

You're not of this world. Or you shouldn't be. Yet, here you are." He splayed his palms as though that explanation meant something to me.

"You'll have to explain a little more in words I can understand," I said. I glanced at the door. It was open. The hallway beckoned beyond. The room wasn't that big. I could make the hallway in four steps and then the front door, which was just to the left, another few short steps away. Ibn would have to run after me from around the other side of the bed. If I was quick, he wouldn't stop me in time to get outside and away, and if there was one thing I knew, I had to get out of here. This whole situation was nuts.

"This is the dimension some human souls come to after they shed their physical bodies. You passed through the veil, young one, but you didn't shed your earthly body. It is still tied to you, and we can't work out how or why that happened. You are neither here, nor back where you should be, which is causing you problems assimilating. Bringing an element of the physical world here with you has never been done before, which leaves me in the rare position of working out how to help you," Ibn said.

My mouth gaped open. "Are you telling me I died?"

He inclined his head. "In a manner of speaking. Yes."

My gaze darted around the room. It looked solid. The mattress under me was firm. My foot tapping the floorboard was slightly cold. I pinched my arm, my was flesh warm. This conversation was crazy. The man I spoke to was even crazier because he spoke as though dying to wake up in a 1930s bungalow was real. "What do you mean 'in a manner of speaking'?"

"That's what we can't work out. You're not of this world, but you're not of *any* world. Technically, you shouldn't exist."

"Yet, here I am." I touched the head band that remained around my forehead. "Why did you put this on me?"

"It was the only way to stabilise you. I thought it might help you regain your memories and integrate into this frequency," Ibn said.

Each time he spoke, a million other questions ran through my empty mind. I dived into the thick soup of nothingness behind my eyes, wincing with another stab of pain. "I'd like you to take it off, please. It isn't working."

"It is working. You might not have regained any memories, but this time you woke," Ibn said.

A chill worked up my spine. *This* time I woke? That didn't sound good. "How long was I out for?"

"Time is meaningless here. Well, not as you might remember it. You were out long enough to worry both Keira and myself," Ibn said, giving me no sign of how long I had been in that white room for. Or here, for that matter.

Again, more questions rammed through my mind than were answered. We were going around in circles and I wondered if Ibn thought he really was answering me or if he was trying to be confusing on purpose. I was through playing games. "Why was the door locked? Why can't I get out of here?"

His smile waned and his brows lowered. "You shouldn't have been able to disintegrate the front door. No other soul has managed something like that. Not without the proper training, that is. It took me some serious manifesting to create something strong enough and I've been practising for quite some time. Now I'll have to redouble my efforts. I should thank you for the challenge," Ibn said.

It was official. This guy was nuts. I slid my other foot to the floor, body tensed to make the dash I'd planned. "You don't have to redouble anything. I'm happy to get out of your hair." *Right now.*

He looked at me with wide, sad eyes and shook his head. "There's nothing more I'd love to do than introduce you to the University, but I'm afraid you can't leave here. Not yet. The house contains your energy somewhat. I must ask you to stay while I work out what to do with you, why you ended up here and if there's another dimension your soul resonates with better than this one."

There was a whole lot of information to unpack and I wouldn't wait around to ask him questions that would lead to more questions. The endless well inside my head surged and pain lanced through my skull. I cried out loud, clasping my hands to the side of my head.

I swayed as I rocked, or maybe the entire room rocked because Ibn's smile vanished and he stood from the dressing table chair, reaching for me, "Easy. Just relax."

I wouldn't take it easy and relax. Not when terror bubbled inside me and the feeling of wrongness stuffed my veins. I was missing something. It was just out of my reach. If only I could remember, but my brain didn't even supply my own name.

A man's face flashed in my mind, and my heart lurched. I had to get to him. I didn't know why, only that I felt compelled to find him with every fibre of my being. My limbs thrummed with the need to get to him. I bolted from the bed, stumbling into the hallway and to the front door.

Thunder rumbled and the house swayed as my fingers wrapped around the doorknob. Energy surged from the centre of my being and curled across the knob and into the wood. I had to get rid of the door. It stood between me and whatever the hell was outside. As I formed the intent, the door splintered into nothingness. I stumbled outside and stopped in my tracks.

Whatever I might have imaged I'd find past the front door, this wasn't it. Instead of a street, or maybe even a front garden, I stood on cold sandstone blocks in the middle of a hallway. Stone arches held a corridor that stretched in both directions on either side of me. A solid wall was to my right, holding many doors in the aged stonework.

A courtyard opened to my left, visible through the detailed lacework that framed the arches. Sunlight danced on bright green grass and hedges of fragrant roses. People sat in groups in the sunshine, chatting and laughing. Relaxed. It was at odds with the urgency that doused my veins.

"You can't go out there!" Ibn called from inside.

I glanced behind my back to see the Professor walking towards me from the open bedroom door. A frown creased his forehead as he strode towards me.

The house inside was a disjointed juxtaposition to where I stood. An unreal reality I didn't want to be caught in so I did the only thing that made sense. I bolted, pushing through the people who walked the corridors.

I ignored their surprised gasps, grateful they shuffled out of my way when I ran past them. They all looked normal, if not dressed a little strangely. They wore a mix of fashions. Some wore togas, others wore long dresses with tight corsets. A couple wore bright clothing suited to the 1960s. I shoved aside the oddness, intent on out-running the Professor who followed me.

I glanced through the open doors, seeing classrooms filled with people listening to lectures. Classrooms filled with people sitting around tables and chatting, open tomes between them.

The scent of fresh flora filled my nose. I peered inside to see a huge greenhouse filled with trees, plants, bushes and flowers that I couldn't identify, stretching into the distance. . It was out of proportion, if the massive fir trees that stretched into the open sky were to be believed. I had to be seeing things that weren't there; losing my mind, at the very least.

"Please stop!" Ibn called, but I was far too scared to listen.

I pushed through a woman and man, stumbling further down the corridor. I glanced into the next room. A group of people stood around a mammoth. Its huge tusks scraped the floor and curved across its head. Shaggy fur trailed over the floor. I'd never seen such a realistic representation when the creature swung its head to peer at me with intelligent eyes.

That's...that was...the animal was... I swallowed over a dry lump in my throat, heart hammering against my ribs. It was alive. The mammoth was alive and people stood around it at ease. Not running from a crazed, terrifying beast that could rip them apart with a flick of its tusks, and what was I thinking - mammoths were *extinct*.

My legs pumped as blind heat ravaged my mind. I stumbled into a stone wall, pushing away. Up stairs. Moving. Running. Stumbling higher and higher until I pushed through a heavy wooden door into sunshine and fresh air.

I wobbled on stiff legs to the stone ledge. The wall beneath my hands dropped way, way down. Acres of lush forest spread into a vast mountain range. A flock of birds scattered from the tips of trees as thunder rolled around me.

Dark clouds billowed along the horizon, obscuring the soft lavender sky. The ominous feeling that prickled through me became pins and needles. My mouth soured and my stomach turned to lead.

Heavy footsteps preceded heavy panting. I didn't have to turn my head to know Ibn came slowly behind me. I didn't run. Instead, my knees wobbled, and I leaned against the stone. There was nowhere to go. Not unless I wanted to drop hundreds of feet into the trees below, or try to push my way back down the stairs to another part of this university that made no damn sense.

There was something about the cloud that made me stare. As strange as this place was, those clouds were not a part of this place. They didn't belong, as though they marred the existence of where I was. Cool notes in the warm air made goosebumps rush over my arms and I rubbed them away as I watched them roil and grow. The forest below grew quiet, leaving only the sound of wind in my ears.

"Why are those clouds here?" Of all the questions I needed to ask, that seemed the most important.

Ibn stopped next to me, leaning against the wall, also staring at the stain of darkness on the horizon. "That my dear, is the question. I have seen many things, but never this. I fear you are the cause."

Chapter Four

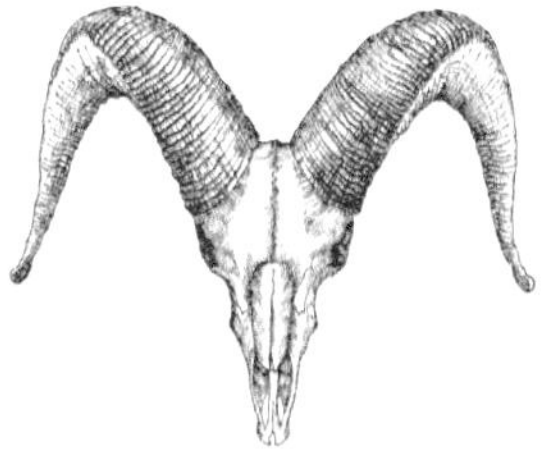

This place wasn't real. *Couldn't* be real, and yet the lavender sky, the room that was a rainforest and the frigging *living* mammoth all told me a different story. I stared at the ominous clouds slowly building on the line of the horizon, blotting out the perfect sunshine from the perfect sky, as a similar darkness built within me.

I was a blank slate, but somewhere within me threw up a belief in the afterlife. The absolute knowledge that once the physical body dies, the soul goes on.

"I'm dead, aren't I?"

Ibn screwed his face. "It depends on what side of the coin you're looking at. Some would argue that this side of the veil is true life, and the other is a playground. A soul is only there for moments. This side is enduring."

I could understand why he'd say that. The forest spread below me teemed with life, the colours more vibrant than I could ever imagine. The building below my feet was a wonder. The people I'd rushed past were real, their bodies solid as I'd pushed past them. If I was in a state of delusion, I doubted my imagination would be this crisp. This detailed.

Besides, I would have imagined something better for myself if I sunk into a delusion; namely a beach, a margarita, and a clue who I was as a start.

My body seemed solid. I still *had* a body, but the world around me wasn't the world I was used to. I didn't have any memories of where I lived, but *that* was a certainty. I rubbed my chest, not able to shake the feeling of emptiness. That there was a vital part of me missing. I winced as sharp pain lanced my head when I dug for the reason.

A gentle hand on my shoulder had me looking at Ibn's concerned face. "Do you need more rest?"

I shook my head, blinking away the pain. I didn't need rest, even though nothing would be better than sinking into oblivion. I needed answers. "I need to know where I am. Who I am."

Ibn clasped his hands in front of him. Despite his strange choice of clothing, his eyes were keen and intelligent, and also filled with excitement and warmth despite the threat of those ominous clouds. "That I can help with. You've come to the University of Creation, where souls learn how to manifest objects from thought. It's one of the closer dimensions joined directly to Earth. It's also the most convenient because souls can manifest there from this side of the veil and help keep the planet, and all souls existing on it, in balance."

I blinked as I stared at him. "You spoke, but made no sense."

Ibn smiled. I wondered if anything might make him lose his patience. "Come back downstairs and I'll explain."

I frowned, glancing at the threat of the clouds. "Aren't you going to do anything about those?"

"I am by explaining to you where you are and why this dimension exists. Changes need to be understood in order to act," Ibn said.

I followed him down the spiral of stone stairs until we came out into the corridor I'd run through. Instead of turning towards the room I'd woken in, he took me down another hallway on the other side of the rectangular garden I noticed was in the middle of the building.

The building itself was huge. The stone craftsmanship was beautiful, reminding me of Oxford University at first glance, and looked just as old. The garden in the between the arched corridor was bright and welcoming. Groups of people sat on the soft grass and chatted in the sunshine. Roses of all colours lined the grass, the warm air fragrant enough to make me want to curl up in the sunshine myself. How long the sun would shine before the clouds obliterated the scene, I didn't know.

"We've been here for four millennia," Ibn said.

"Pardon?" My attention snapped back to the strange Professor.

His smile was understanding. "Most people want to know how old the building is. This was the dimension originally set up to use Earth as a playground for creation before human souls wanted to manifest there."

I stopped short, forgetting to walk. Ibn paused, turning as though surprised I'd check out with news of that magnitude. My mouth fell open and closed a few times before I spoke again. "But the Earth is older than four millennia." That was if my high school science was to be trusted.

Ibn waved his hand in the air. "Time works differently there. In fact, time isn't a consideration. It's really only a construct for Earth. When I say four millennia, I mean we've just been here for 'now'. I only say that for the newly arrived to understand we precede human souls manifesting on Earth."

Again, his timeline was out, and I couldn't stop myself from telling him. *Was being precise part of my personality?*

"According to National Geographic, humans have lived on earth for three hundred thousand years."

Ibn's eyes twinkled. "We've been manifesting on Earth since the very beginning."

"But...there were no people in the very beginning." As far as my knowledge went, there was only primordial soup. Homo-sapiens came much later after evolution had a chance to work.

"And what makes you think souls have to take human form to manifest? A soul doesn't have to manifest in its entirety to experience life on Earth. We can dangle our fingertips, as it were, into lesser physical bodies to experience how it feels to be in that body, to live that life, however long that may be."

My blank mind spun. I didn't understand why I knew nothing about myself, but I could recall general history at will. What he said made little sense. "Do you mean to tell me you've been a fly?"

"Yes and a flower, too. Although in that instance, I existed as a mere passing thought. No need to go through the rebirthing process for that. Souls only go to those lengths for progression and growth," Ibn said.

"Do you mean to tell me...what I mean to ask is..." My mouth stuttered to a stop along with my feet. I couldn't know for sure, but I think Ibn was telling me the secrets of the universe in the same way as asking me if I would like a biscuit with my tea.

"You want proof, yes?" Ibn said.

"You have to admit, this is very hard to take in," I said.

Ibn's smile softened. "You have shed your physical form and your soul has come to where it resonates. *Normally,* a soul would shed its physical body before finding its resonance time after time. You're somehow still joined to it. The body is merely the vehicle to exist on Earth. The soul exists before the physical body. It has to. One cannot manifest without existing prior. However, in your case, I'm unsure."

Ibn's frown didn't make me feel any better. Nor did his explanations stop my questions from forming. "Time after time?"

"Of course. The soul doesn't stop seeking to grow. To experience life in all its forms. You my dear, have lived many times," Ibn said.

"How do you know?" I asked. If I had shed my physical body, then surely I would have regained my soul's memories from various lifetimes. "How can you be so sure?"

"Those are the questions I will show you proof of to answer," Ibn said.

I followed, as Ibn walked along the corridor and rounded a junction. My mind spun with everything he'd told me. I had no way of knowing if it was the truth or if he was delusional. Both choices seemed equal, but I had to find out what he meant if I wanted questions answered.

We walked along a winding path until we came to a building resembling a church that was as big as the building we'd just left. The constraints of physical law didn't work in this world. I was sure we hadn't walked far enough to come from the massive university to another building of this size.

Spires reached for the sky, white clouds swirling around the tips. I had to tip my head back to see to the top. I couldn't hazard a guess at how large and tall the building was. It was simply *massive*. Its walls stretched as far as I could see to my left and right. Stained glass windows framed by ornate arched windows shed shapes of oranges and yellow light onto the bright green grass. A pathway on grey gravel ran down the length of the building and housed a trimmed garden of small bushes containing delicate purple and white flowers.

Ibn walked up several steps leading to a huge arched doorway made from gleaming dark wood. As he approached, the door swung open of its own accord on silent hinges, opening to a dark interior.

Warm, musty air surrounded me as I followed Ibn inside. I found myself at a cross-way made from inlaid wood. An aisle stretched too wide and long for me to see to the end. Flying buttresses arched overhead, holding up a vaulted ceiling made from light grey stone. Flaming sconces flickered on the columns, creating a flood of warm, honeyed light inside.

Instead of seating, as I thought would be in a church of this size, row upon row of shelves stretched from floor to ceiling. Books of all widths, sizes and colours crammed onto the shelves.

"It's a library?"

"Don't let the outside fool you. The building is the latest manifestation by a group of students. They modelled it from the Cologne Cathedral. Gerhard von Rile taught the manifestation. I guess you can tell by the style," Ibn chuckled.

I couldn't tell by the style, nor did I know who Gerhard von Rile was. All I could do was stand in the middle of these books feeling completely overwhelmed. Ibn noticed. He came to me and held my hands as though he understood the confusion swirling in my mind. I wondered if anything could worry him. He seemed so unflappable. "Fear not. We're here to find your akashic record. I hope that by reading about your lives, it'll jog your memory."

Again, more questions filled my mind, even when he tried to explain himself. "What's an akashic record?"

"The best thing is to show you. Come, we'll find your room," Ibn said.

My room? I had a room here? That couldn't be possible. But then Ibn was off, striding through the centre corridor and turning into a gap between the shelves. I'd lose him for sure if I lost sight of him. I jogged to catch up with him to see him half way down a narrow aisle.

The sheer number of books was overwhelming. I tried to calculate how many there might be, but I couldn't hope to guess. The dimensions inside the building didn't match the look of the outside and I felt as though I were in an Escher painting.

I glanced at some titles as I passed, coming to pause when I read: Eighteenth Life as Hippocrates, 460 - 372 BC.

"What the…?" My feet came to a stop, and I reached for the volume before I realised what I was doing. The book was light, weighing a fraction of what it should, given its thickness. The cover was beautifully inlaid with embossed golden lettering and a detailed design to frame the same title as was on the spine.

Sucking in a breath, I opened the page. The insides reminded me of a bible, and the way monks of centuries ago hand wrote and illustrated the pages. The craftsmanship was stunning, but what drew me in the most was the content. I traced the word with a fingertip that resonated deep inside me.

A wise man should consider that health is the greatest of human blessings, and learn how, by his own thought, to derive benefit from his illnesses.

I knew those words. They welled within me, strong and clear, seeming to me a way of life. The sensation of something just out of my reach washed through me, followed by a sharp crack behind my eyes. The books blurred, and the tome dropped to the floor from my nerveless fingers.

My senses swam back into focus to find Ibn kneeling next to me. I was crumpled on the floor, the book I'd held open beside me, several pages folded beneath it. I reached for the book. It was too lovely to damage. "Oh, no!"

Ibn picked it up. He smoothed his hand over the paper. After his hand passed, the crease disappeared.

"How did you do that?" I asked, my head pounding.

"It's a simple manifestation, too. I will the damage gone and it is done," Ibn said.

I tried to shake the fuzziness from my head, but didn't succeed. "I hope one day I'll understand what you're telling me."

Ibn cupped my elbow and helped me to my feet. I swayed, exhaustion tugging my limbs. "Surely I shouldn't feel this way."

If I were a soul, I couldn't get tired. Only physical bodies grew tired because they needed to sleep. Eat. Rest. That was all supposition, of course. There was no way of knowing. There was no way of knowing *anything* because my mind was a confused mess.

Ibn blinked concerned, warm brown eyes at me. "You should be in perfect health. The soul is eternal. I fear your situation isn't getting any better."

I had to agree. My heart turned in my chest when I saw genuine worry on his face, an emotion that had been lacking since I'd first laid eyes on him. I spoke around a tongue that was too thick. "What will happen if my...situation...doesn't get any better?"

"This has never happened before, but..." Ibn sighed. "The dimensions are interlocked. If one fails, it will upset the others, and..."

"And?" I swallowed down a dry throat, not wanting to know the answer, yet needing to hear it all the same.

Ibn focused his brown eyes on me. "And all levels of existence will implode."

Chapter Five

One soul couldn't have such power.

"God." The word fell from my lips as the full force of everything settled hard and cold in my stomach. "Are you sure? I don't want to doubt you, but how can that all tie to me?"

I had to believe he was wrong. Or this was one hell of a nightmare. If it was, I wanted to wake the hell up right now. Only I didn't wake up and Ibn simply returned the book to its place on the shelf.

"That is what I hope to find out in your records. If there is a key to understanding why you passed without shedding your physical body and why you have such power draining your soul, it's there," Ibn said.

"Then why do we have to go to a room? Why aren't my books here?" I gestured to the thousands of books on the shelves. The thought of rifling through so many of them was an impossible feat.

"These are the lives souls have devoted to the public development of humanity. They decided not to live a private life before they descended, and as such, their lives are available for anyone to learn from," Ibn said.

A headache thundered beyond my eyes. I rubbed my eyes, caught up in weariness and confusion. "I wish I had aspirin."

"Here."

I blinked open my eyes to see Ibn holding out two white pills and a glass of water. "How did you...?"

"Dimension of creation, remember? Whatever you want, you can create," he said.

I took the pills and threw them into my mouth. The water was cool and soothing and I gulped it down, giving myself time to think. A drip fell from my bottom lip to the hospital gown I still wore. "What about some new clothes?"

"Think what you want. See it clearly in your mind and create some," Ibn said.

I eyed him. Nothing made sense since I'd woken up, but the thought of some better clothes appealed. I sighed, closed my eyes and tried to imagine clothes I might wear. Having no memory, I was surprised when my mind supplied familiar jeans and a t-shirt.

"You're a natural," Ibn said with a smile in his voice.

I staggered when I looked down at my body, seeing the gown gone, replaced by the jeans and t-shirt I'd imagined. I flattened my palms on the material, gaping at the feel of denim and soft cotton. "How...?"

"Dimension of creation, remember? There has to be a reason you came here," Ibn said, before leading me away.

Although my clothing had changed, the band around my head remained. I stumbled after him, realising the glass of water had disappeared when he stopped at a wooden door in the middle of the bookshelves. It had no reason to be there.

Behind it, enormous shelving units and books stretched into the distance. If these were the 'public lives', my mind reeled to understand how many 'private lives' had been lived.

Ibn opened the door and we stepped into a cosy room that had no right being where it was. A fireplace crackled at the end of the space. Three comfortable-looking leather couches surrounded the fireplace, set out in an arch to face the flames. A window looked out over a garden, filled with flowers, neat lawns and blue sky.

Shelves, which rose to waist high, filled the rest of the room. Five double sided shelving units were on each side of a central aisle, covered with more books. Some were quite slim, while pages stuffed others. Some spines were colourful, while others were made from aged leather and golden gilt writing.

"There's so many." I calculated a rough estimate, coming up with about two thousand volumes. "Do you think we have to go through every one?"

"Some people do when they first arrive. It helps to align the memories left behind in order to go through the cleansing process to incarnate when they feel the need, but in your case, I don't think we'll have to," Ibn said, gesturing to a plinth on which sat a book at the far side of the room. "The room has provided."

I followed Ibn down the aisle to the book made from soft, brown leather. Embossed with gold on the cover were the words *Life of Marie Stone*.

Marie Stone. The name rolled inside my head. Familiar, yet not. I ran my fingertips across the title, my forehead tightening with a frown.

"Open it, my dear. This must be important for the room to emphasise this life in particular," Ibn said.

My stomach rolled when I opened the cover. A hand drawn portrait of a smiling beautiful woman opened on the first page after the cover, with the words: *Marie Grace Stone. 1902 - 1935. Wife to Elliot. Mother to Benjamin.*

I looked to Ibn. "Are you telling me I'm Marie?"

"In one of your lives, you went by the name of Marie, yes," Ibn said. His gaze roamed my face, no doubt looking to see if anything twigged.

I looked back at the portrait. "I don't remember anything."

"Come. Sit. Read. Memories often require a bit more information to reattach than the first page," Ibn said.

I picked up the book, which looked slimmer than some others. Going by the dates, she'd only been thirty-three when she passed. *So young.* I wondered how much she'd accomplished in thirty-three years. If she'd been happy. What challenges she'd faced, and why she'd passed so young.

My heart fluttered as I sat on the couch, gripping the book with tight fingers. The leather swallowed me. The crackling flames were soothing, their gentle heat seeping into my cold skin. They helped get me under control, and I wondered if that was their purpose. If all souls who read about their past lives suffered from the same weight on my shoulders.

This was supposedly my life. Or one of them, if the many books behind me were to be believed. I didn't feel as though I'd lived so many lives. If I had, surely I'd feel more knowledgeable. Older. Wiser. Just...*more* than the blank brain I was now. Taking a deep breath, I opened to the first page and read.

Marie's childhood seemed normal. Loving parents. Full family life. Emigrants from England who set up a new life in Melbourne. What her family lacked with money, they more than made up for in love.

It was all normal enough stuff. That was until she began full-time work when she was seventeen. Marie was hired as a secretary to a Police Chief, heading up one of the largest precincts in Melbourne. At first, she was afraid. Melbourne had a healthy underbelly, but the chief took her under his wing and protected her from coming face to face with the worst of them.

Until the day he asked her to take notes for a trial he had to attend. He didn't want to ask her, but she was the fastest typist and she couldn't decline. She was tied up in knots the night before, and didn't get a wink of sleep wondering about the trial, and the criminal she'd met.

Unfortunately, it was one of the worst. Joseph Theodore Leslie 'Squizzy' Taylor stared at her with small, blank eyes as he declared himself not guilty for the accessory to murder, amongst other charges.

Marie couldn't believe her ears when Taylor was found not guilty of conspiracy, but was relieved when the criminal was convicted of a less serious charge of occupying a house and sentenced to six months in prison.

It was at the Melbourne precinct Marie met a beat cop by the name of Elliot Stone, who had worked to convict Taylor. She recognised his soul the moment she laid eyes on him. Her soul had found her home. A wisp of longing wove through me. Hers? Mine? I wasn't sure.

I sat back and stared into the fire, thinking of Marie's life. That all seemed pretty normal to me. Meeting the person to form a life-time bond with was common, but when I continued reading, the next paragraph stole any warm fuzzies that may have settled in my chest. Elliot was a...Light Stream worker? What the hell was that?

I was drawn from the flickering flames as an image of a face formed in my mind. The face was handsome. Male. Cutting jaw, straight nose, sensual lips and piercing green eyes. The type of green that reminded me of cut gems. Emeralds. It wasn't just the colour that made my heart roll. It was the intensity of that stare. The fight and determination and unwillingness to give up. They called to me, those eyes. I *knew* this man. Knew him like I knew my soul. He was a vital part of me. He was...

Agony sliced through my head. I doubled over, hot bile rising in my throat. The band around my head vibrated. I clenched my eyes tight, not finding the solace behind my closed lids I wanted. I wasn't going to give up. That man. I needed him like I needed my next breath.

Elliot! His name was Elliot! And he...

My gut twisted and lurched. He wasn't here. He was missing, and I...

He should be at my side. He should always be at my side. We can only be complete together. A promise was made. Long ago. Yet to fulfil. He and I...

White hot agony lanced my skull as my fingers clenched the immovable band. Images unravelled in my mind, flickering in a nauseating rush. A jeering face filled with contempt and malice. Another face overlaid, sublime and beautiful. Golden curls that framed sea-blue eyes. Eyes that looked at me with desperation before the light dimmed from them forever. As the man died, demons swirled around me, lacing me with sharp claws. Images pounded my mind, overlapping one upon the other, jumbling into an untidy heap in my mind.

A ruby, red as blood sinking into my skin, simmering deep within me. Becoming me. Turning me into something '*other*' and then fracturing...Pieces of my mind tearing apart and scattering into a dark void.

Thunder rolled through the room, making the books and furniture rattle. I looked through the window to see the blue sky obliterated with darkness. A dark shadow sped past the window, barely a darker part of an inky cloud. Blazing white light followed. The light morphed into a humanoid shape, with huge feathered wings spread behind him. A golden sword gleamed as though lit from within and slashed downwards by a muscled arm, slicing through the shadow. The room rocked as though blasted from somewhere deep below the ground. I clung to the couch, and the book slipped between my knees to the ground.

Ibn raced to the window, fingers clutching the sill so hard they turned white. "No! It can't be. This isn't good. This isn't good at all."

I wanted to ask what couldn't be, and why the man who couldn't be worried was so distressed, but all that came from my mouth was a dry wheeze. Footfalls thumped outside the door.

I spun, nearly slipping from the seat of the couch, in time to see the door fly open. Several gigantic golden figures stepped into the aisle, dwarfing the shelves of my books. They pulled white feathered wings tight to their backs and slid their swords into sheaths behind their heads as they strode towards us.

My mouth fell open as I stared at them. Made from marble, their white skin stretched tight over bulging muscle. Golden light glowed from within, giving them an otherworldly look. Hell, they *were* otherworldly. Fine platinum hair fell below their shoulders, some braided, some hung loose, floated around their faces and brushed by an invisible wind.

Their faces were achingly beautiful. Chiselled by a master hand. The kind of flawless beauty that was only dreamed about in the minds of master craftsmen, but never fully able to yield. Yet, here they were. Utter perfection.

The male who led the small group came onto one knee, his massive thigh muscles bulging as he moved. White sandals adored his feet, the laces climbing over chiselled calf muscles. He wore a white pteryges of firm leather. A wide belt cinched his waist, inlaid with fine strands of gleaming gold.

Bands encased both wrists, the leather embossed with beautiful, delicate patterns that shimmered with pearlescent light as he moved. The man, male, angel, celestial being looked at Ibn, his electric blue eyes glowing. "Professor, those who do not belong have breached this dimension. The doorway between our worlds is collapsing. We need your light and knowledge to restore before all is lost."

Chapter Six

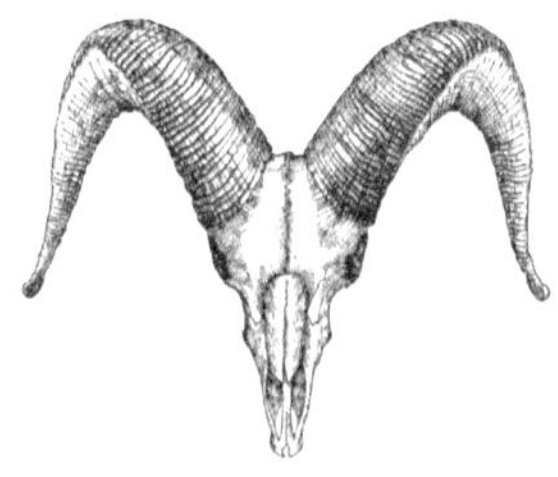

Ibn stepped towards the angel. "General Saniel, what has breached our veil?"

The angel had a name. Saniel. And he was an angel general? Saniel stood unflinching and the epitome of an otherworldly being used to fighting. Power strummed through his body and I could well imagine that the being led an army of angels. "Demons and abominations that shouldn't exist. I've never seen such creations. They're plucking souls and devouring them. Feeding on them."

Pain spiked through my mind. I gasped, clutching my head as their name came to me, "Soul-eaters."

More images flew through my mind. Horrible memories alongside a jeering face. I recoiled, slipping from the seat as my equilibrium canted sideways. Warm arms caught me and lowered me to the floor.

"Do you know these soul-eaters?" Ibn asked, his brown eyes filled with concern.

"I...think so. I remember them. They..." My mouth turned sour as fractured images flashed through my mind, alongside a name. I clutched Ibn's tunic as a stone formed in my stomach. "Black John."

Ibn helped me to my feet and went to the last book on the closest shelf. "It's too soon to open these pages, but we don't have a choice."

I glimpsed the name on the cover. *Cassandra Hunter. Born 1987.* There was no death date, and I frowned as Ibn opened the book and flipped through the pages. He strode in front of the fire, fingertip tracking down the pages as he searched.

The name felt familiar. Memories bubbled up somewhere in the back of my mind, the pressure compounding as they pushed against an invisible barrier that could have been a mile wide. My head pounded, seeking the freedom that wasn't coming.

I knew what soul-eaters were. My heart fluttered as I relived the memory of a dark shadow devouring a man crossing a road right in front of my eyes, and another stealing the existence of a young boy rounding the front of a bus.

The souls that soul-eaters devoured weren't only eaten. They were snuffed out from existence and somehow this Black John was connected.

Saniel's hand rested on the pommel of his sword. "Professor? If the doorway collapses..."

Ibn shared a horrified look with Saniel and I wondered what would happen if the doorway collapsed. It was clearly nothing good.

Ibn flipped the pages, his movements fast and determined before he tapped the page. "Here it is."

A shiver stole through me at the dark tone in his voice. I stood to read what he'd pointed out, but he snapped the book shut before I could see a word. "It's best if the memories of your last life were to return naturally. In your state of mind, I fear it could permanently damage your fragility if they were forced."

Permanently damage my mind?

Before I could ask the multitude of questions that swirled in my head, Saniel asked, "Have you found the answer, Professor?"

Saniel's brilliant gaze slid from Ibn back to me. My breath stuttered under the full impact of those ancient eyes.

"Soul-eaters were created in the grey-mists by a dark soul. How that soul obtained such power is a question for another time. Technically, these soul-eaters shouldn't even exist. Their creation has even escaped my knowledge," Ibn said, his gaze drifting over my face.

Lines framed his mouth, and he shook his head as he turned his attention to Saniel. "Because they are abominations, they can tear irreparable holes between the veil. Not just our veil, but all of them. The rules don't apply to them. The doorways can collapse if they aren't stopped. Saniel, they have the power to destroy even one such as you."

Saniel offered Ibn a curt nod. His eyes hardened as tension strummed through his body. "Understood. We fight to destroy or be destroyed."

I flinched at his words, said as though he could be talking about the weather. The general was either brave or stupid. That was harsh. He was an angel. He didn't think the same way as a human soul, so I wondered how I knew that epiphany with such clarity.

Ibn sighed. "I hate to destroy any form of life, but removing them from here is imperative, General."

Saniel sent Ibn a curt nod. The angels wasted no time and strode from the room, taking the weight of power around them as they went. I breathed a little easier and watched through the window as Saniel and his army shot upwards into the thick of the soul-eaters, their movements so fast they were streaks of burning light.

Shadows swarmed them. Angelic swords glinted as they slashed through the demons and soul-eaters invading this world. Black clouds roiled behind them as though fighting to suffocate the land and everything in it. Including us.

I staggered to the window, fingers clutching the frame. Some lights blinked out. "Oh god. Oh no!" I wheezed, watching as more beautiful lights - *angels* - were taken from existence.

"I need to oversee the battle," Ibn said. His face was etched in lines, ageing his timeless face as he came beside me.

"I'm coming with you." I was involved in all this. Although I didn't know why but I couldn't just stay here watching from inside a room.

"It's safer if you remain here, my dear," Ibn said.

I couldn't be stuck away here while total destruction took place outside. No amount of reading would help anything if it was all destroyed, and what would anything matter if it was. The timeless knowledge of countless lives might be eradicated forever. "It's not safe anywhere. I'll come back later. There are more pressing issues."

Ibn set a weighted look on me, and I knew he wouldn't relent. I grabbed his elbow and walked us both to the door. I wasn't giving him a choice as I hauled him out of the room. My skin itched with the need to do something. Anything. "Come on. You can tell me on the way what a bad idea it is that I come."

Ibn sighed, but set a course along an aisle lined with ancient tomes. I wouldn't have been able to do a thing if he really didn't let me come, and I also knew enough to know he wouldn't have let me come if there wasn't another reason. I just had to wonder what he'd read in that last book he'd picked up, and why there wasn't a death date for Cassandra Hunter.

And if Cassandra Hunter was really me.

I rolled the name in my head. It was familiar in a way that was on the tip of my tongue, but nothing snapped into place in my mind. The barrier holding off my memories grew higher, more impenetrable, and then it lost importance as we stepped outside.

I was sure it took longer to get to the room with my books, but a few corners later and we stood on the same steps we'd entered the building. The scent of ozone and sulphur stung my nostrils. Shrieks and deep growls thundered around me. Golden light flashed as the angel army fought deep shadows. The ground rumbled and booms cracked through the sky.

I staggered, hands clutching my ears as visions of another time, another battle, reared through my mind in which a giant demon destroyed a massive building in front of my eyes. Bloodied bodies were strewn across the ground, detritus of their terror and failed escape surrounding them. A briefcase. A shoe.

People were with me. People I cared about, one meaning more than life itself and terror unlike I'd known raging through me. Pain slashed through my head as I reached for more of that memory and I fell into a dark pit inside my mind.

My back arched, and I came onto my toes, arms outstretched as power surged through me, locking bones, sinew, muscle. My body exploded with light so bright that emanated from deep within, it illuminated the whole side of the building and the gardens. Ibn gasped, shading his eyes with his hand as my light blasted him.

An electric current surged inside me, my veins filled with lava as energy surged, burned under my skin as it looked for a way out. Black shadows dropped from the sky, charging towards us so fast that in moments I saw the black holes that were their eyes and gaping mouths filled with unending darkness. Their clawed, bony fingers stretched towards me, their tips razor sharp.

Angels fell from the sky, racing after them, but they were too far behind. A soul-eater slashed its claws through the roof of the building, sending chunks of stone and tile through the air as it demolished the building.

Another building demolished in the same way passed through my mind, then the impression of a man's face. A name followed. Elliot. The loss of something so great it felt like half my chest was with him shocked me, chased by fury. These creatures had stolen something infinitely precious to me.

This was going to end. Now.

The energy strummed inside me, coalescing as I formed the thought, bent to my will with intent.

A soul-eater lunged from the roof of the building and dove down on me. Blinding white light shot from my forehead, encasing the soul-eater. The light devoured the soul-eater in moments, leaving nothing behind when it disappeared.

An angry screech shrieked, incensed. Soul-eaters hailed towards me. I should be scared. I should be *terrified*, but power surged inside me, numbing anything I felt until there was one focussed thought. Annihilation.

My consciousness raced out of my body, surging upwards and outwards. The life in this dimension brushed my awareness as I flew past. I raced past pockets of reality teeming with life. Human souls. Angelic souls. Souls that were other. I was aware of them all until I reached a pinnacle where every pocket of life and reality surrounded me before I snapped back into my body with the force of a bomb.

Light streaks exploded out of me, shooting in all directions towards the soul-eaters and demons, lighting them up with unerring accuracy. The light engulfed them, flared and snuffed out, leaving nothing but faint wisps of white dissipating smoke. The remaining soul-eaters and demons fled and retreated into the black clouds.

The clouds surged, churning and pulsing, before recoiling until they hovered on the horizon. Wisps of black smoke drifted across skies that were dull and flat, as though the energy had leached away, stealing the clear blue it once was.

My power stuttered and dispersed, leaving me cold and shaking. I collapsed onto my hands and knees gasping for breath. Agonising pressure built inside my skull. I cried out, clawing the sides of my head as though that could take the pain away.

I needed something; the other part of my soul that would complete me. I desperately wanted the man who filled my head and my heart with longing, although I didn't understand why. My broken head threw up his name. Elliot. I wanted Elliot. I wanted his arms around me. I wanted his comfort. His safety. His love. I didn't remember him, but my emotions were a map towards him. I locked onto them with both hands as though that could force the memory from my fractured head.

I cried out as power stuttered to life again, but much weaker than before. Burning pain lanced my head as light glowed from my forehead, growing larger and brighter. A silhouette stumbled towards me and the light vanished around him.

He looked around, his brow creasing in confusion until he saw me. His breath hitched and familiar green eyes flared as I became his entire focus. He stepped towards me. One step. Two. As though not believing that it was me.

"Cassie, is that... is that you?"

His honeyed-whiskey voice sunk into my skin like a sigh. His fingers ploughed through my hair as he drew his cheek against mine and caged me in his arms. He breathed in deeply, filling his lungs with my scent as my trembling fingers clutched him back. "Cassie! My god. I can't believe...how...why?"

I had no answer to give, but then it didn't matter when he held my face in his gentle hands and crushed his lips to mine.

Chapter Seven

"Where have you been, Cassie? How are you here? *Why* are you here? Thank God you are!" Elliot wrenched his eyes off me, glancing at Ibn, the church and the shaken people who wandered in from the gardens before coming back to me, still keeping me in the steel cage of his arms.

The logical part of my mind knew this was Elliot. I recognised his face from the fleeting flash of memory. He was a stranger, yet here was no mistaking the deep longing that had brought him to me.

His fingers ghosted over my cheek, and his other arm banded about my waist. He kissed me again as though he couldn't help it, as though he had no choice about it. His tongue slid languidly into my mouth, taking liberties as though he'd kissed me a thousand times before. Maybe he had, but I couldn't remember.

I sank into his embrace, my body curving against his as his lips moved on mine. He deepened his kiss, a tremor working through his hands. "I thought I'd lost you, Cassie."

His voice was deep and rough, filled with anguish. My heart twisted with an answering wrench, wondering what I'd done to cause it.

"I..." There were no words. No explanation. Just an unending sludge of nothingness. I wanted to do anything I could to take away his anguish and I feared I would only cause him more.

His brows pulled low and a deep groove formed between his brows. His fingers stilled on my jaw. "What is it, Cassie? What's wrong?"

I searched my mind for something - *anything* - I might remember, but everything inside my head was a jumbled mess. Pain seared behind my eyes. I gasped, wincing, my hands gripping a head that felt it was exploding.

A scuffle sounded next to me, and Elliot's arms firmed about my waist, using his body to shield mine. "Stay away from her!"

I squinted through bleary eyes to see Ibn easing away from me. "I mean no harm."

"Who are you?" Elliot demanded.

"It's okay. He's a friend," I said.

The force of golden angels landed on the with rubble strewn lawn. Saniel strode towards me as he sheathed his sword in the scabbard between his enormous, powerful wings. His blazing eyes landed on me. "How did you do that? How did you spear them with such powerful light?"

"I...I don't..." I looked up at him through streaming eyes. There was no explanation. I only knew that my veins flickered with power that came to life with a thought. As though, for that moment, I *was* the power.

"That is the power inside her," Ibn said. "Such power. Too much for your soul to handle." His eyes flared round in shock, his face pale.

Elliot scooped me from the ground, holding my shaking form in his arms. He set me on my feet, winding a muscular arm about my waist as though he couldn't bear to let me go. I didn't want him to. His body heat wrapped around me. I rested my pounding head against his shoulder, wrapping my arms around his waist as a sigh rippled through my body. This was safe. This was home. If there was any right place for me to be, it was here no matter where I existed, whole or not.

Tension thrummed through his body as his arm tightened. His fingers flexed around my hip. "You can stay away from her, too," Elliot said.

Saniel's stern features hardened as he looked Elliot from face to feet. "How did you cross dimensions, interloper? The veil can only be traversed through doorways, yet you broke through, just like the soul-eaters."

Elliot wasn't an interloper. I'd manifested him. Wanted him. Called for him. The power had responded and brought Elliot to me. I was getting a sense that this wasn't supposed to happen.

Saniel looked two seconds from running both of us through with that huge golden sword behind his back. I'd seen how fast he could move. If he decided to do that, we wouldn't stand a chance. Electricity picked under my skin, melting some of the chill away. Saniel's gaze slid to me, as though he knew what was happening inside me.

"I don't know how I came to be here, but I can only thank god I got out. Where I came from - Hellioth - it's falling apart," Elliot said.

"Hellioth is falling apart? How is that possible?" Ibn stepped towards us, his forehead creased.

Elliot glanced about, taking in the dark sky, the destruction and shaken audience we attracted. "Lilith has taken it over."

"The clouds brought the soul-eaters and demons." The rolling black clouds spiked another jab of pain in my head, along with a sick feeling that weighed down my stomach.

"There's something about them. I think I remember, but..." I winced at another jab and gave up trying to search my mind.

"The clouds are how the soul-eaters and demons cross dimensions. Lilith worked out a way to use them to break through the veil. She's creating an army with plans to take over all dimensions. She's already succeeded where I came from. It's also how she invaded Earth. The darkness was her manifestation all along."

The name Lilith was a faint shadow in my mind. Passing through but dispersing when I tried to latch onto it. "Lilith?"

Elliot's frown grew deeper, and I had the urge to smooth the line between his brows away. "She abducted me when we went through the portal. I've been going out of my mind wondering where you were ever since. I thought she'd stolen you, too. I couldn't find you anywhere."

"I came here," I said, although I hadn't exactly worked out where here was.

"Thank god you did. Lilith's demons threw me in a dungeon. I couldn't escape. I couldn't do anything to get to you," Elliot said.

"A dungeon?" Horrified, I took in the stains on his white shirt and scuffs on his pants. His hair was dishevelled and limp, more so than usual, since he had a habit of running his fingers through it. "You run your fingers through your hair. A lot. I remember something about you!" I smiled, happy I recalled that about him.

Elliot's fingers firmed about my waist and he tilted his head towards me. "What do you mean, Cassie?"

I shook my head, unable to describe the state of my mind. I knew I should know Elliot. I had a life book about him. I knew I should know a lot of things, but everything was white noise in my head.

"She can't remember who she is, or her past lives," Ibn said.

Elliot's fingers swept hair from my forehead, his fingers stilling on the band. "What's this?"

"It's the only way I could help Cassie. The power is too great for her soul. Without it, she will degenerate," Ibn said.

Elliot's horrified gaze roamed my face. My stomach turned and twisted. I knew my state of mind was unusual. "Is this true, Cassie?"

I clasped my hand over his and squeezed, trying to comfort him even though my heart felt it was racing out of control. "At least I know my name now. And I know you're called Elliot."

"That's it? That's all you remember? Not Thomas, nor even Ben?" Elliot said, his voice only a rasp.

"Those names were in the book Ibn had me read," I said. I recognized them. "Ben was Marie's son and Thomas was her grandson."

Other than name recall, I didn't understand who these men were. I knew as a son and grandson, Marie would love them, but to me they were only names. I swallowed, even though my throat felt like it was closing over. It was important that I know. That I understand. I cried out when I dug into the mess inside my head.

With a strangled sound, Elliot folded me against his chest, his heart pounding. "Oh, Cassie. Oh god, Cassie. This is worse than I thought. Worse than anything I could imagine."

Tears stung my eyes. I tightened my hold on him, anchoring myself to him even though my head ached. I closed my eyes through a bout of dizziness. "Tell me about them. Tell me what I should know. That will help me remember. Please. Tell me everything."

"You should remember everything now you're through the veil. You should have all of your memories," Elliot said.

"She didn't shed her physical body. I tried to work out how to help her," Ibn said.

"Ibn helped me, but everything is fractured. Please, Elliot. Tell me who I am." I wasn't beyond pleading, desperate now to understand the truth about myself.

"I had her read one of her life books. I thought it might have helped, but I think I've only succeeded in making her mind worse," Ibn said.

"You showed her an akashic record and she still didn't remember?" Elliot asked.

Ibn shook his head. "She wasn't reading for long before the demons attacked."

"She shouldn't have had to read it at all." Elliot's horrified stare bored into me.

He drew in a deep breath as though to steady himself. "Ben and Thomas incarnated with us, along with others, like your mother, your father, your sister, as you know them in your life as Cassie. They're part of our soul group. They're souls who have chosen to serve us throughout lifetimes. They're Light-Stream workers, Cassie. Just like you and I."

Ibn drew in a sharp breath and Saniel shifted his weight. I glanced between the two. They knew that term too, it seemed, and I...I recognised it too!

The breath stalled in my chest as I clutched Elliot's wrinkled shirt. Images of ancient biblical artefacts flashed through my mind. Tables and cases filled with them. Light-Stream workers were so important, but I couldn't remember why. Or how. Pain stabbed behind my eyes. I shuddered, fighting the urge to vomit as a wave of nausea rolled over me. I squinted at Elliot through my watery vision, his grip on me telling me what he was going to say was important.

"Lilith knows who we are. *What* we are. That's why she trapped me, Thomas and Ben there. She's taken over the dimension and sealed it. Nothing gets in or out. She wants to control all dimensions and all life, but she needs more power to do it," Elliot said.

Elliot's emerald gaze darkened. I squinted into his face through watery tears, a feeling of doom turning my intestines into knots. "She knows where to get that power, Cassie. That's why she attacked this dimension."

"That much power is in this dimension?" My gaze bounced between Ibn, Saniel and Elliot, finding no answers other than the sickening dread that turned my stomach to stone.

A muscle worked at Elliot's jaw. "It is, Cassie. You are the power that's fracturing you apart. Hadriel gave it to you with his dying breath and she saw it all. You have the power to open all the portals between dimensions. You are the master of it all. Lilith won't stop until she gets what she wants. You."

Chapter Eight

"Hadriel...is dead?" Saniel gasped. His normally severe features grew slack. The angels standing behind him murmured in shock. Their collective grief constricted around me.

"He protected the power of the portal as best he could. Lilith was going to steal it from him, but he sent it to Cassie instead. He protected it as best he could," Elliot said.

Saniel's gaze slid from the ground to lock onto me. He squared his shoulders and fell to one knee. He bent his head, his huge wings held tightly to his back. It was one thing seeing this powerful angel standing tall and proud, and another on his knees before me.

"Please, get up, Saniel," I said.

He lifted his head, his electric blue eyes glowing, and remained on his knees. "I will serve you, Lady."

I frowned, looking down at Saniel. The title felt familiar, but it washed over me, leaving me with an endless pit of dread in my stomach and a spinning head. I clutched Elliot's shirt, helpless to know what to say or do. My legs shook with the strain of simply standing. I leaned into Elliot, grateful when he supported me so I could stand. My skull pounded, and I didn't want to go digging into my mind again, knowing the pain it would cause.

"I don't want him to kneel." It was wrong somehow. I didn't need anyone kneeling before me. Especially not an angel General.

Sleep called for me. My body throbbed with a deep ache that wouldn't go away and all I wanted to do was lose myself in darkness in Elliot's arms and forget this mess. I closed my eyes, inhaling Elliot's scent, letting it soothe me.

Elliot stroked my hair. I leaned into his touch, needing it. Some of the aches eased, but I was exhausted. The energy I'd used left me weak. "She needs rest. Is there anywhere familiar I can take her?"

"Yes. I manifested a room based on her past life. All indicators showed it was the best place for her to assimilate." Ibn's voice sounded faraway.

"Let's get her there." Elliot swept me off my feet and cradled me. I sighed and relaxed into his body heat, curling into his chest without any hesitation.

"You know her soul. Can she be helped?" Ibn asked.

Elliot's grip firmed around me before relaxing. He sighed and his breath ruffled my hair. "I'll do everything I can to make sure she's safe."

I was safe in Elliot's arms, but I didn't know what Elliot could do to help me. I was in a worse state now than when I first awoke here. It was only a matter of time before more than my mind fractured.

"We'll secure the perimeter of the cloud while the Lady rests, and keep the demons contained," Saniel said. Wings snapped as the angel army took to the skies, taking with them Saniel's ancient energy. My eyes closed and it would take too much energy to open them again.

"Where is the room?" Elliot asked.

"I'll take you there now," Ibn said.

I dozed as Elliot carried me to wherever Ibn led. Their footfalls sounded on stone before a door opened. Elliot huffed and stilled as he stepped through a doorway. "This is where you said she felt safest?"

"This is the space," Ibn said.

The moment stretched. "I can see why my soul-mate chose this place to awaken in," Elliot said.

Soul-mate. Yes. That's what we were. My mind rang with clarity. The knowing undeniable. We were soul-mates. Two halves of the same whole. We were destined to be together.

"You are her soul-mate? I can see why she called you to her. It must have taken great power to tear you two apart," Ibn said. I cracked open too-heavy eyelids to see Ibn watching me with concern.

Elliot nodded. "Lilith is very strong. The Light Stream workers imprisoned her on Earth for millennia, but she broke free. If it wasn't for her, we would have passed through dimensions together."

Not even life, or death, could keep us apart. The words filtered through my mind, ringing with truth.

Ibn let out a sigh. "As her soul-mate, you should be able to heal her, however I fear with Hadriel's power, it may not be enough. I'll seek the help we may need."

I silently agreed with Ibn. I'd taken some soul-eaters out of the equation, but some remained, hiding in the darkness. Ibn left and the door clicked shut behind him. Then it was just myself and Elliot and thoughts of soul-eaters and demons flew from my mind.

I cupped Elliot's cheek with my palm. "My soul-mate."

Elliot's eyes flared. "Yes. Soul-mate."

I saw the ageless look in his eyes now because I recognised it. Lifetimes of experience shone from their depths with unrestricted access to vast reservoirs of knowledge. Heat flared in those emerald depths. There was an answering tug in the centre of my chest.

"I've always been here for you, Cassie. I'll always be here for you," he said.

My thumb rasped across the stubble of his jaw. I knew his words were honest because they couldn't be anything but as the truth rebounded through a connection that bound us together.

"I need you," I said.

Ibn closed the front door behind him with a soft click, leaving me with Elliot in a living room with two stuffed armchairs nestled before a fireplace. A memory flashed through my mind of myself and Elliot kissing in front of a crackling fire.

My core throbbed at what Elliot and I had been doing in front of that fireplace. We hadn't merely kissed. We'd come together in an explosion of need and frustrated yearning. Images rushed through my mind, too fast to decipher.

I kissed Elliot, but he wasn't this version of Elliot holding me. That Elliot had been dressed in a suit of armour. A jagged scar ran from his temple to his chin, vivid against his pale skin. This Elliot had dark hair and tanned skin, but there was no denying the tenderness etched on every line of his face.

Another memory overlaid knight Elliot. This Elliot had long, straggly blond hair and was a giant of a man with broad shoulders and thick thighs and a wolf skin folded across his shoulders. He removed it and wrapped it around my waist as he drew me towards him before thoroughly kissing.

More versions of Elliot flickered, one over the top of the other. Elliot dressed in a tartan kilt, then near naked except for his loincloth. Then he existed as a man in ragged, stained clothing. Then a woman wearing a powdered white wig. Next he had dark skin, then tanned skin, then pale skin. Asian. Indian. African. All nationalities. All versions were with me. Kissing me. Loving me.

I sensed others surrounding us. We were some sort of group. Souls that burned as bright and that held as many different bodies as Elliot.

As me.

The shards of memory were disjointed. The sharpened edges dug into my skull when I tried to see who these souls were. I cried out as the world spun around me. The band around my head vibrated with heat.

"Shh. Relax, Cassie," Elliot said.

I shook, my breath heaving in too-tight lungs. My fingers dug into Elliot's shoulders. He pressed his lips to my forehead, not caring that beads of sweat dotted my skin. My heart rate eased. The whirlwind of memories faded to a dull ache. Elliot's fingers brushed the hair from my face, his touch the balm I needed.

I focussed on his touch. It centred me. *He* centred me. The invisible band around my chest eased, allowing me to draw in a deep breath. His scent filled my chest unleashing a throb of heat. I clenched my thighs, rubbing my nose against his neck, locking to his familiar scent. No matter how many faces and how many bodies he'd inhabited, his scent didn't change.

I let the soothing balm of his presence roll through me, happy that the pain normally stabbing my skull had receded to a dull ache. As long as I didn't push trying to glue the fractures back, I could cope. At the moment, I wasn't interested in fragments or demons or portals. I just wanted the calm that Elliot gave me.

"I'm here for you," Elliot whispered, his nose nudging my ear. I shivered with his promise and also the touch of his skin against mine, floating in the calm. A bond trembled beneath the mess in my head, small but there. I reached for it, clinging onto it. My mental storm instantly rolled away, leaving space to think. To feel. To *be*. My mind was a grateful blank. Tears sprang to my eyes, grateful for the respite. In the calm, ancient awareness seeped through my awareness.

A river of knowing replaced fractured images. The awareness held no memories, but the knowing was steadfast. I knew with an absolute sureness that we were connected.

Intimately.

My soul recognised his, no matter what body he wore. What he looked like was superfluous to the ancient connection between us. That bonded us together. He'd always be here for me and I for him. How or even why, I had no idea. Only that it *was*.

My head had finally quietened and I wanted to take advantage of it. I wanted him. Needed him.

"Kiss me," I whispered.

"With pleasure," Elliot said.

He captured my lips with his, kissing me deeply. Our lips moved together as though we'd kissed millions of times, naturally, purposefully. The residual pain in my mind slipped away to nothing, allowing my desire to ignite.

I clung to his tall frame as he walked through the house. He lay me on a soft mattress and followed me down, stretching next to me, before collecting me in his arms and crushing me against him.

"I was so worried for you, Cassie. While they had me locked in that dungeon, I dreamed of holding you like this," he said.

I didn't want to think of Elliot locked in any dungeon. My fingers curled over his shoulders as he rolled me on top of him. "Let me help you forget about the dungeon. Let's forget about everything except the two of us."

These moments of not knowing were all there were. I had no past. I could only live in the now. I canted my hips, rubbing my core against his hardness. Delicious sensation spiralled through me at the intimate contact.

Elliot groaned, his eyelids dropping as he gazed at me. "Do that again and you're going to fry my brain."

I liked that idea. I leaned down, capturing his lips, pulling his shirt up and over his head. My eyes skated over a vision of hard muscles and smooth skin. He was lean, but well-formed and strong.

I grazed my fingers across his broad shoulders, between his pecs and down the valley of his torso. A breath stuttered. "Do you like my form? I can change anything if it displeases you."

I gasped, realising I'd lost time exploring the dips and ridges of his body. Did I like his form? My mouth watered at the sight of his flesh. Yes. I very much liked what I saw. Nothing about him displeased me. What I felt must have been clear on my face, because Elliot said. "Touch me all you want, Cassie. I am forever yours, in any way you may want me."

His voice was thick and warm and set my blood on fire. Elliot cupped the back of my head and laid me down to kiss him again. He slid his tongue between my parted lips and I met each slide and caress of his tongue with one of my own. His fingers threaded through my hair and splayed his palm across my lower back. The heat from his hand seared my skin and when he rolled his hips, forcing his hardness against my core, I jerked as delicious sensation spiralled through me.

I moaned and melted against him. I couldn't help myself. I needed to feel his skin on mine. I skimmed my hand over his shoulders and down his trim waist. Over every defined dip and ridge of his torso. He was all hard edges and velvet skin over firm muscle, and I couldn't get enough of him.

I kissed his mouth, across his sharp jaw, to the pounding artery in his neck. I licked his skin, moaning at the explosion of salt and spice on my tongue. Elliot moaned as I kissed my way across his collarbone and pressed my lips over his racing heart.

"Cassie, what you do to me?" he rasped. His fingers tangled in my hair, before he skimmed both hands over my shoulders and back as though he needed to touch me everywhere at once.

I shivered with the pleasurable thought. I'd like that too. The same insatiable need coursed through me. If I didn't touch him all over, I would somehow combust. As though I had to touch him to make sure he was really here.

I shifted, my fingers brushing his pant clad hip before stroking his hardness. Heat seared my palm as my hand found his length. He jerked hard enough to shake the bed when my fingers curled around his shaft. In my hand, his erection was a steel bar far too covered for my liking.

I moved back to perch on his solid thighs to unbutton and unzip his pants. His hands stilled on my thighs, fingers flexing. His breath heaved as his body stilled. I stared at the expanse of his chest to find his gleaming eyes on mine. "How I've dreamed of your hands on me. Dreamed of being with you like this for decades. Not existing in a half state as I was, but really here. With you. Now"

I heard the ache in his voice, the weight of his words. "Decades?"

His hands brushed up my arms so lightly it caused me to shiver. "It was nothing, my love. I would've waited millennia for you."

He'd waited. For me. For decades.

He'd wait for *millennia*.

Holy. Hells.

There was no more waiting. If we'd waited decades, we'd waited enough. My fingers skimmed slowly across his hips as I parted the material that hid him from me. He throbbed as I revealed his length, his shaft pulsing with need.

My mouth watered as I traced his erection. A drop of liquid emerged from the tip of his throbbing shaft. His cock twitched with each beat of his heart, velvet over steel.

"Cassie, I...ahh..." His mouth fell open as I curled my fingers around his length.

His heat seared my skin and liquid fire raced through my system. This man. This beautiful, caring man who had waited for decades for me was coming undone at my touch. His chest heaved, and his fingers flexed as I stroked him. He held as still as he could, letting me explore his body, knowing it was something I needed to do.

Touching wasn't enough. I needed to taste. I scooted back and leaned down. The first swipe of my tongue along his shaft made us both groan. My core grew slick as I parted my lips and pulled him into my mouth.

His taste exploded on my tongue. I moaned, my body alight with liquid need as I licked and sucked. I rolled my hip as my urge built inside. His fingers tangled in my hair as his hips jerked as my movements became more urgent. I gripped his shaft, swallowing as my need burned deep. He throbbed in my hands, in my mouth, and as my desire crested his fingers gripped my arms. He uttered an urgent sound, pulled me away, flipped me onto my back and reared over me, eyes blazing, veins throbbing in his neck.

A growl rumbled from his throat. "Enough, Cassie. Although I enjoy your mouth on me, I need more of you. Now that you're in my arms and we're where we're meant to be, I can't wait any longer. I'm going to have you, and I'm going to have you now."

Chapter Nine

I moaned as he dropped a hard kiss on my lips, filled with the same need that coursed through me. Liquid need coursed through me as his kiss trailed from my mouth and over my jaw. This was what I needed. Blind, exquisite desire made my body throb with need.

I was a writhing mess as I tipped my head back and exposed my throat. He pressed his lips to my throat as he ripped my shirt from my body. I gasped as cool air hit my skin, but I wasn't cold for long when his mouth found my breast and suckled my nipple. Hard.

"Elliot!" My fingers flew to his hair. He knew exactly what I needed. What I couldn't ask for.

"I'm going to help your memories return, Cassie, and then you'll see how magnificent you truly are," Elliot rasped.

He palmed my breasts, his mouth working lower. I writhed beneath his urgent touches, too fogged with need to go slow. He gave me exactly what I wanted. How I wanted it. Only he could quench this all-consuming desire pulsing through my body and obliterating my mind.

My thighs parted as he settled between them, his fingers working the button on my jeans. My fingers tangled with his as I helped him and worked the garment off my hips and legs.

Wet heat doused my core as Elliot took me in his mouth. I screamed as an unexpected orgasm raced through me, my back arching off the bed. White haze fogged my mind as I peaked. My body tingled as he laved my seam and swirled my clit with the tip of his tongue. I fell back to the bed, a panting mess, but he wasn't finished.

"You're beautiful, Cassie. So damned beautiful!" Elliot whispered.

The power of his words settled into me, soft as a sigh. I felt their truth and honesty matching something inside me. I reached for him. "Make love to me, Elliot. Please."

He grinned, his eyes lighting. "You don't have to ask me, Cassie. I would make love to you every hour of every day if you'd have me."

He stood from the bed and removed his pants. His hand circled his cock and my abdomen tightened. Fresh wetness coated my thighs.

"Come to me, Elliot Please." I needed him on top of me. I needed him inside me. Desperately.

He squeezed his hard length as he devoured me with his eyes before he crawled the length of my body, hovering above me. "Anything for you, Cassie. Anything."

My core throbbed as I grabbed his shoulders and pulled him to me. His hips settled between my thighs and we both groaned as his hot flesh met mine. He slid his cock through my wet folds, canting his hips, teasing as he kissed me.

My body sang with the rightness of our intimacy, but I needed him closer. As close as he could be. I tilted my hips and caught his tip at my entrance. Something snapped into alignment within me.

He moaned as he eased in, his delicious length filling me. My eyelids fluttered closed as he settled inside my body, his length throbbing inside me. My internal nerves raced with tingles that spiralled throughout my body.

Elliot pressed his cheek beside mine, breathing heavily. He kissed my neck, nibbling the sensitive skin before he slowly pulled out and thrust back inside. I jerked as sensation released in an exquisite burst before he eased out and thrust back again.

I clenched his shoulders, my thighs crushing his hips as he teased me. My stomach tightened as I hovered on another precipice. Elliot drove into me again, this time pressing down on my clit with his pelvis, and I saw stars.

My mouth opened with a silent scream. Every muscle locked as I flew back into the delicious white fog that consumed me, and I soared through another climax. Elliot kept pressure where I needed as I hovered on the periphery of my consciousness in a place where our bond thrummed with pulsating intensity.

I reached to touch our ancient connection. Images unfolded in my mind. Different lives. Different ages. I saw the children we had. The parents who nurtured us presented through images and scenes that had no sense of belonging.

People who I should recognise - but didn't.

I floated back to my boneless state. Elliot's eyes gleamed with heat and satisfaction when my eyelids fluttered open.

"Are you back with me?" He asked in a thick and heat filled voice .

I nodded, unable to find the words I needed. He kissed me deeply, his tongue sliding into my mouth before he rose on his elbows on either side of my shoulders and moved once again.

He thrust into me, and tingles spiralled through my sensitive flesh. His pelvis met my thighs with a firm bump that jolted my body. This was no soft easing of his body. No teasing to send me into an orgasm. This was Elliot using his body for us both to find release.

I gasped with each pounding thrust, clawing his shoulders, wrapping my legs around his hips just to hold on as he slid in and out of my core. My next climax built, a coil winding and tightening deep in my belly.

Elliot's thrusts grew harder, more urgent, uncontrolled. I held onto him as tightly as I could. I spiralled upwards, muscles tightening, inside snapping, Elliot slammed into me, grinding himself against my core. His cock pulsed and my insides filled with heat. His body bowed over me, eyes clenched, sinew standing out on his neck as he groaned.

I spiralled upwards again, another orgasm racing through my system, losing myself in the white haze. This time there were no people. No images. Only smooth, calming whiteness enveloping me as I soared before I floated back.

Elliot wrapped his arms around me, pressing me against him. His heart thundered in his chest as he rolled onto his back, taking me with him. He arranged my legs, settling me on top so that we remained intimately connected.

His breathing evened out as he stroked my back and pressed a kiss to my temple. He brought his arms around me, his heart beat pumping under my ear. "I've made love to you for millennia and always it's like the first time."

My breath stuttered and I flinched. The warmth from making love drained from my body.

"What is it, Cassie?" Elliot tipped my head back to look into my face.

I didn't know what to tell him. He spoke as though I should understand who he was. Who I was. He thought I should remember, but I didn't. My vision turned hazy as tears filled my eyes. I tried to blink them away before he saw, but of course he noticed everything.

Elliot's brows lowered, his face creasing in concern. "You don't remember." He didn't need to ask.

I eased off his body and sank to the mattress next to him, chest tightening, stomach churning. He reached for me, but the coldness in my blood made me stiffen. He didn't let me go. Instead, he captured me in his arms, his body tight against mine. Instead of closing me in, it made me feel safe. As though my broken mind wasn't mine to bear alone.

I drew a shuddery breath, clasping his arms. "I..." The words stuck in my throat and I couldn't get them out. Heat built at the back of my eyes and my throat tightened. A sob broke past my lips and then I couldn't stop.

He held me as I cried. I shuddered with each body-jerking gasp of breath. I cried, waking to a nightmare. For not knowing who I was. My past. For not remembering a man who clearly adored me and *I didn't even know who he was.*

"What's wrong with me? Why can't I remember?" I sobbed.

His hand firmed on my back. "I don't know, but...we'll work it out."

I hoped he was right and that there was a way, but right now, I didn't see one. I sniffled against his chest. The need to know who I was burned like a fire inside my chest. I was sick of having nothing but an empty black hole in my fractured mind. Hated knowing we were soul-mates and yet all I had were dissociated, disjointed images that *meant nothing.* "Tell me who I am, Elliot. Please."

I was desperate to know. To understand. He moved a strand of hair from my tacky face and tucked it behind my ear. "We came together millennia ago when we were young and naive, to incarnate with an agreement to help our souls grow. Not only you and me, but those of our soul family, although we only chose to be with one another as intimately as we are. You and I have lived over a thousand lifetimes on every continent on Earth, in every time of history. Rich. Poor. We've aged and also died young. But we don't only incarnate for our soul's growth. There's another, even more important reason, for our existence."

Elliot paused, weighing his words. His gaze filled with the aeons of his experience. Times that I didn't remember. A niggling voice whispered in the back of my mind. What if I never did? What if these lives I didn't remember living would never come back to me? What if I'd lost them forever? We'd lived lifetimes together. Shared experiences that no two other souls ever had. If I didn't remember, would I also lose Elliot?

The tiny line between his brows deepened. "Whatever you're thinking, it's not going to happen."

"How do you know what I'm thinking?" I asked.

A soft smile touched his full lips. "Didn't I just tell you we've lived lifetimes together? We know each other inside out, Cassie, and I can tell when you're chewing yourself up on the inside. I'm here for you. I'll always be here for you, no matter what. A bit of memory loss won't deter me."

"But..." What I felt was more than a bit of memory loss. The inside of my head was divided by chasms of nothingness, and agony stopped me from trying to piece it all together. I might never get my memory back. I couldn't ask him to stay by my side and nurse me. Not after he remembered over a thousand lifetimes, and I remembered nothing.

He placed a finger to my lips. "We've been Egyptian royalty and lived as primitive tribes people. We've starved, hunted, killed and lived in wealth. We've stolen, and been victims. There are always trials to overcome in life and between lives, but the main thing is that we've always faced things together. This isn't anything different, and I'm afraid that this is another trial of our true calling."

He sucked in a deep breath and it was my turn to frown. He hesitated. Why did he hesitate?

"You remember when I said we're both Light-Stream workers?" Elliot asked.

My blood ran cold as I nodded. The term was familiar, even though I couldn't recall the details. "I remember."

"When we incarnate, it's our job to protect biblical artefacts gifted to the earth by angels. These artefacts are extremely powerful and are meant to be used for the progression of humanity, so that any souls incarnated can grow and not stagnate. Because these artefacts are so powerful, they're attractive to beings who seek them for their own gain. These beings are not necessarily human souls.

"Entities cross dimensions to claim these artefacts. To some, the power is too great a call. It's our job to protect them and to make sure that they're used as the angels intended. It all went a bit pear-shaped in my life as Elliot."

My brow pulled into a frown. I didn't like the sound of this. "Pear-shaped? How?"

He traced my jaw, my cheek, my bottom lip with his fingertip, as though he didn't want to tell me. Now I really didn't want to hear what he said. "When we incarnate, we don't keep our memories. We're born with a clean slate. We grow up, live our lives before we're inevitably found by other Light-Stream workers and trained." He huffed. "Sometimes it would be easier to keep our collective memories, but that would defeat the purpose of learning and growing. It's arranged that we meet others tasked with the same objective.

"During my life as Elliot, an artefact fell into the wrong hands. I wanted to bring this criminal in and make him pay for his life of crime on Earth. It was my job. During an investigation, Black John found out about my duties as a Light-Stream worker. I was double-crossed by this man and my partner."

I gasped, my hand flying to my mouth. "No!"

Elliot's lips twisted. "They murdered me for the artefact. When I left my body, I went straight to find you. In that life, you lived as my wife, Marie."

That was the name in the Akashic record Ibn gave me to read. "Marie was murdered too," I said.

Elliot nodded, his face etched in sadness. "You were murdered by Black John before I could get to you and your soul had already passed the veil. You'd probably thought I'd already passed. Black John somehow trapped me in the grey mists before I could follow you. I was cut off from our home dimension and I lost my memories. My sense of self. I lost everything that made me who I was, until you called me in your life as Cassie."

"How did I do that?" I asked. "If a soul is incarnated, surely they can't see other souls."

"That's true. But you chose to come as one of the sighted, I think, to find me. You must have known I was trapped when you returned and incarnated in a way that would find me." He clasped my arm, a tremor running through him. "You did that, Cassie. You found me and saved me."

I broke into a smile, clasping his hand. "I helped you?"

"You did. But it set a series of events in motion that no-one could foresee, and I think Lilith orchestrated all of it. She had millennia to plan her escape, and she used her time well." His gaze turned dark. A muscle ticked at his temple.

"How could she do that? You said she was imprisoned?" I said.

"She was, but she must have worked out a way to escape. She used the power of angels. We set some free, but they're still trapped on Earth and in the dark-mists. She used their power to break free from her confinement, but she needed to draw out one of the most powerful angels to open a portal to her dimension."

Elliot sat up, swinging his legs over the side of the bed. He ploughed his fingers through his hair, making the strand stand out in all directions. I sat next to him, wrapping a blanket about my shoulders. The heat from his body melted into me. "What happened, Elliot? What did she do?"

Elliot turned his head to look at me and I flinched at the bleakness in his eyes. "She wanted Hadriel for his power, but he transferred his power to you with his dying breath. I thought I could help stabilise you because we're soul-mates but I didn't. If you remain fractured, there's nothing stopping Lilith from taking it from you."

I leaned into him, needing to touch him, the draw towards him undeniable. "Maybe if she has this power, I'll get my memories back. Surely after our lifetimes we'll think of another way to stop her."

Elliot's gaze was bleaker than before. "You can't give her Hadriel's power. Cassie, she has to kill you in order to take it. She'll take the power. She'll take your soul. She'll take *everything*. If she gets her hands on you, there's no way you'll survive."

Chapter Ten

My fingers clenched the blanket I held to my chest. Tense muscles replaced my languid state. Maybe I was a fool for allowing myself to relax, but the temptation of Elliot had been too great. I would not beat myself up about making love to him, no matter how bad his news was.

I knew of Lilith. My battered mind at least gave me that. A dark shiver raced down my spine. History had painted her as a demonic spirit who devoured infants and children, the first wife of Adam and the devil and queen of hell. She apparently got around. She was many things, but the actual truth was darker and uglier.

She was the true queen of hell. She'd been one of the first souls to incarnate as a human soul, however through her deeds she'd lost any light her soul once had. She'd grown so dark, so evil that she could no longer incarnate on Earth and had been relegated to the darker, lower vibration dimensions where she thrived. If she had her sights set on me, Elliot was right.

I wouldn't survive if she caught me, power or not.

I massaged my temples, my fingertips brushing the band cemented around my forehead. I was pretty sure that was the only thing keeping me from total insanity. "What can I do, Elliot?"

Elliot took my hand in his. "*You* will not do anything. *We* will plan something and keep you safe. And just for the record, I'm not losing you, Cassie. I'll do everything I can to fight Lilith. She's not taking you away from me."

In a way, she'd already taken so much away from me. My memories. Lifetimes of experience gone as though they were dust, however inadvertently it may have happened. I was nothing but an easy to control blank slate. I couldn't access my life experience as a Light-Stream worker, and I couldn't access Hadriel's power.

I curled my fingers around Elliot's wrist. "I wish I could remember you," I whispered.

Elliot stood, drawing me to my feet. "Don't think about that now. Come with me."

He led me to the bathroom and started the shower. He kissed me while waiting for the water to warm before drawing me inside with him. He turned me around and washed me with tender brushes of soapy hands.

"Relax, Cassie. Don't think of anything," Elliot rasped.

He kissed me as he cleaned, pressing his lips to my shoulder, my arm, and the centre of my back. This was heaven. My eyelids drifted shut and my head became too heavy to keep upright. Elliot placed my hands on the tiles, sliding his wet, soapy hands down my waist and hips.

"So beautiful," Elliot whispered. His hands brushed over my thighs and calves before drawing higher. My core throbbed, needing him to touch me where I burned.

"When I was trapped in that dungeon, all I could do was think of you. I hated not knowing where you were. Hated to think I couldn't reach out and touch you."

His fingers swirled softly on the soft skin of my thighs, slowly caressing higher. I widened my stance, pulsing with need. My lips parted in a whine. His fingers traced the edge of my lips, too lightly. I wanted more. I jerked with each teasing touch, my blood simmering with arousal.

"But then you called me to you, Cassie. Deep down, you know how to use the power. You can call it to you. Lilith wants the power because it's stronger than you, but you are more powerful than her," Elliot said.

His fingers slipped through my wet folds to my entrance. He dipped his fingers inside me. My forehead fell forward onto the tiles and a moan tore from my lips. I panted as he played with my clit and drove me higher when he impaled me with his fingers.

He pressed against me, his hard cock nestled in between my buttocks as he curved over me from behind. He grabbed my hip with one hand, while he stroked between my thighs with the other. My fingers fisted as my abdomen tightened. My core throbbed. Empty. Too empty.

"Whatever body you take, I know it. You're as familiar to me as my own body. Your soul is the perfect balance to mine. If I say that we'll find a way, then we will. Look inside and you'll see the truth, Cassie. Lilith is not only coming for you, but she's also coming for me. We're in this together, and together we'll fight her," Elliot rasped.

"Please, Elliot. Please," I whispered.

I arched my back as his fingers sunk into me. I writhed and pushed against his hardness, needing him to fill me with his fingers.

"Feel me, Cassie. Look inside and you'll see me," he said, plunging his fingers inside me and pressing the heel of his hand on my clit. I soared, an orgasm crashing through me.

My legs shook as Elliot gently stroked my core. I would have fallen if not for the support of his body.

"Please. Please. Please," I chanted into the wall. I wanted more than his fingers and he didn't make me wait.

He gripped my hips and lined himself behind me, easing into my sopping core. I cried out, my internal nerves sensitive as he invaded my body, drawing the length of him so that his thighs met the back of mine.

"Feel me, Cassie. Feel me with your body and your soul," Elliot said. He gripped my hips, eased out of my body and thrust inside me again. I jolted against the tiles with the force of his onslaught.

I groaned as I spiralled. Each lunge taking me higher, making me lose control. My moans echoed off the tiles over the harsh slaps of flesh meeting flesh. His hand slipped to my clit and he pressed down as he thrust into me.

I shattered.

I soared through the white haze into a part of me that knew no time or boundaries. I was nothing and everything. White light broke into bright coloured shards, racing towards me and away from me and a presence rose beside me.

Masculine. Familiar. Love.

Elliot.

He wove around me, making me crest higher in euphoria. There were no words. No memories, but they weren't needed. My soul blended perfectly with his. His essence brushed against mine. I knew and understood every facet of his personality. His wants. Needs. Desires.

His soul was so, so beautiful.

I wrapped myself around it, surrounding myself in its perfection before I drifted to my body. Elliot's arms were about my waist, his chest pressed tightly to my back, his face against my neck. He breathed hard and his heart raced, each beat vibrating into me.

"I felt you, Elliot," I whispered.

"And I, you," he said.

"It...it was..." No words could describe the perfection of his soul. Or the loving energy that had embraced me.

"I know."

Elliot kissed my shoulder. I trembled as sensation spiralled through me, leaving me bereft as he eased himself from my body. He washed us off before turning off the water and wrapping me in a fluffy towel. His green eyes gleamed and I saw the spark of his soul in them. Now that I saw it, I would always know what to look for.

Someone knocked on the front door. I jumped, startled, taking in Elliot's grim expression. "I think Ibn is back with the help he promised."

My stomach plummeted. Making love with Elliot was only an oasis of time. My fingers found the immovable head band and I wondered how much worse I would be if it were off. Would I already have fractured apart?

I was still naked from our shower. I wondered if I could dress as I'd done before. I closed my eyes, a floral dress passing through my mind. Air whispered around my body and I found myself in a light blue dress with a cinched waist that fell to mid-calf. Dainty pink roses dotted the light and warm material.

Elliot's pants were light grey, tailored and high-waisted. His white shirt was rolled to his elbows and set off with a striped light grey and black tie. A dark grey fedora graces his head and set off his deep eyes and full lips.

"You always loved to wear that dress," he said.

I brushed my palms over the skirt. "I did?"

Elliot nodded. "You were Marie in that life. You wore it with a matching blue cardigan when the weather turned cold."

My cheeks heated at his smouldering look as his eyes lit up with appreciation. "Maybe there's a part of me that remembers our lives together."

He brushed his knuckles over my cheek. "You wouldn't have chosen those clothes without some part of yourself remembering."

Lightness wrapped around my heart. His words had given me hope. A little hope was all I had, and I was going to grab onto it with both hands. Someone knocked at the door again, more urgently.

Elliot's lips turned down, and he folded my hand in his. "Our time is up, Cassie"

I let him lead me from the bathroom. My feet were filled with lead, every step making me feel I walked to my doom. Elliot opened the door to find Ibn and the woman who'd been there when I'd first woken, Kiera.

Ibn's brows rose. "I see you're feeling better."

"Unfortunately, our soul-mate bond wasn't enough for Cassie to regain any memories," Elliot said.

My cheeks heated further. I may not have regained any memories, but I couldn't regret what we'd shared. The try had been worth it. As though sensing my thoughts, Elliot glanced at me and his lips twinged.

"I believe I may have found some help," Ibn said.

Ibn and Keira followed us through to the living area. Keira held a cloudy crystal globe as she perched on the arm of a chair. Her clear blue eyes found mine. "This is an inter-dimensional crystal. It should let us see and talk to Hanniah, from the light-mists."

I peered into the globe. White clouds swirled within the sphere, moving with an invisible wind.

"Hanniah?" I asked.

"She's the highest of angels. Guardian of guardians to mortal souls," Ibn said.

Keira caressed the globe with her hand, disturbing the clouds. Blue skies parted beneath the clouds, to be swallowed up again. A frown formed on Keira's forehead as she palmed the crystal.

"Is it normally this cloudy?" I asked.

She shook her head. "No. It's usually clear and all we have to do is touch the crystal to speak."

Ibn paced the room, which did nothing to soothe my fraying nerves. A bead of sweat trickled down the side of Keira's face as her jaw firmed in concentration.

"Come on," she whispered.

Finally, the clouds swirled, leaving a patch of blue. Sunlight beamed from beyond the clouds, throwing silvery streams into a flawless blue sky. A face formed from the sunshine, morphing into a beautiful woman with cascading dark hair, alabaster skin and plump ruby lips. Ibn moved next to Keira and peered into the globe.

Elliot looked over their shoulders. "Hanniah!"

My eyes flared, surprised that Elliot knew the woman.

Her smooth forehead crinkled as she looked through the crystal with concern. "Welcome friends, but our communication is being blocked."

Ibn nodded. "This is why we're contacting you. Hadriel gave his power to one of your Light-Stream workers, and I'm afraid Lilith is attempting to steal it from her."

Hanniah gasped. Her frown deepened as she worked through the news. "The master demon escaped?"

"Yes. I don't know how. I didn't know until she showed herself. She's using the protection of a mortal body to remain hidden from you, even though she's separated from Earth. She never showed her true face when she imprisoned me," Elliot said.

"She imprisoned you? Where?" Hanniah asked. Her voice separated into a chorus that churned with anger. The clouds in the globe writhed and flashed with lightning.

"In Hellioth, one of the dark dimensions. She's also imprisoned Thomas and Ben. I only escaped when Cassie opened a portal and brought me through," Elliot said.

Hanniah's blue eyes found mine, piercing me with ancient power. She stared at me so intently, I stifled an urge to fidget. Her eyes missed nothing, seeming to see right into my soul. Something pulled in the middle of my chest, bringing a chord deep within me and tugging it outwards. I gasped, flinching at the strange sensation.

"Dear gods. Cassie," Hanniah whispered. Her mouth parted and pity creased her face.

I clenched the material at my chest in a white knuckled grip. That kind of pity I didn't want. "Do you...do you know me?" I asked, stepping closer to the globe.

"My dear one, you are one of my protectors, as is Siel," Hanniah said.

Confused, I turned to Elliot. Hanniah had looked at him as she'd spoken. Elliot smiled. "Siel is my original name. My name when I'm not incarnating."

"But you let me call you Elliot," I said.

He nodded. "I didn't want to confuse you. You were comfortable with the name Elliot, and I let it be."

"But, I..." The name Siel meant nothing to me. My stomach hollowed out, and I clenched the sides of the chair. Throbbing pain skirted my conscious mind, and I knew if I delved any deeper, it would pounce on me.

Elliot stood in front of me. "I didn't mean for it to hurt you, Cassie. Calling me Elliot isn't a lie. It's still the truth. I will answer to all names you call me, just so you know."

I licked dry lips. "Do I have an original name?"

His entire face lifted in a smile. "Amirel."

My chest stuttered. I rolled the name in my mind, meeting a wall of unending darkness. It meant nothing. Absolutely nothing. I refused to give into the well of hopelessness threatening to eat me alive.

"Cassie." Hanniah spoke, using the name I knew was mine at least. "You didn't shed your mortal body when you came through the veil."

Elliot cursed under his breath. "I wouldn't have agreed for you to come with me through the portal if I'd connected with my full memory. At the time, I didn't know it would put you at risk. I thought only of Lilith."

I shook my head, reaching for him. "It's not your fault. None of this is your fault. Please...don't blame yourself."

"If only I'd known...if only I'd..." He swept his fedora off his head with one hand and ploughed the other through his hair.

"Cassie is correct, Siel. You suffered from the grey-mists. You had no way of knowing what the outcome would be from the other side of the veil," Hanniah said.

I didn't like Elliot blaming himself. It was wrong he'd taken on responsibility. "The way I see it, the only person to blame is Lilith. We have to work out what we can do," I said.

"You must shed your mortal body on Earth. You must reclaim a part of your soul left with the physical. Hadriel's power is great, but some of it remains attached to your body in that part of your soul. Unless you have fully passed through the veil, you will continue to fracture," Hanniah said.

"Then I'll shed my body," I said. I didn't understand why they all looked so grave. To me, it seemed to be the only answer, and if it meant my mind would heal, I'd do anything.

"We freed some angels from the dark-mists, Hanniah. More are still imprisoned there. Demons also escaped onto the Earth plane and there's no way of knowing what's happening there with the clouds trapping us here," Elliot said.

"This is worse than I thought," Hanniah said.

I looked to Elliot for clarification, not understanding how this was all connected.

"We can't pass through the cloud barrier to get to Earth unless you can create a portal, but if you somehow do and you shed your mortal body, then you forfeit staying on Earth unless you go through the rebirthing cycle. If you do that, you'll go through the process of forgetting and will be reborn again. We won't be able to free the angels nor fight the demons that are in danger now. And right now, the other members of our soul group are in danger of being destroyed by soul-eaters while they remain on Earth," Elliot said.

My head spun, trying to connect the dots and coming up with one great big mess. "So you're saying there's nothing we can do?"

Elliot's mouth firmed into a straight line. "I'm saying that we're going to have to make the best of bad choices, because bad is all we have."

I looked at Hanniah through the crystal. "Surely there has to be another way."

She had no time to answer. The ground shook and an explosive boom vibrated through the room. The clouds in the crystal whitewashed the globe. A crack split the sphere and it shattered into tiny shards and scattered onto the floor.

A shriek rent the air and an entire wall of the living area disintegrated with another rolling boom. The dust didn't have time to clear before massive black figures swarmed through the hole and descended on me.

Chapter Eleven

A massive clawed hand encircled my waist and I screamed. The pointed ends tore through my clothing, wrenching me from my feet to slam into the demon's hard bones. Sulphur singed my nostrils and stole my breath.

"Cassie!" Elliot cried, voice hard and wild.

The lizard part of my brain reacted. The part that was stuck in survival mode, and enabled me to stare death right in the face and respond by fight or flight. I'd love to have the option of flight, but the claws popping through my skin didn't give me the luxury of a choice. I kicked and lashed and screamed, becoming that type of prey that was too much trouble to catch. The demon was having none of my antics. He was too strong and too fast. It whipped me from the living room and then we lifted from the ground and swooped into the sky.

The stringent scent of sulphur filled my nostrils, choking me. Tears streamed from my eyes, but through my bleary vision I still saw that we flew towards the roiling black clouds. A township was way down below, the streets leading into forests and beyond into fields.

I couldn't let the demon take them through those hostile clouds. The power. I had to use the power. Deep down, I was stronger than the demon. I closed my eyes, digging inside, trying to reach for it, but all I felt was my heart pounding a way out from my chest.

Come on, you can do it. But I didn't know how I used it before, or how I could draw it out past the terror clogging any part of me that could save me.

A flock of demons surrounded us, trapping me in the middle of throat tightening horror. One of them clutched Elliot, body limp, shirt spotted with blood. His head lolled on his shoulder as the wind whipped his hair. *Oh god. Oh no. They had him too*!

I clenched my eyes closed, delving for any scrap of power that might flicker free, but it was locked inside me in an inaccessible part inside too scared to raise its head. I knew how it felt, but it wouldn't shut me out. I needed that power, and I needed it now.

I cried out, teeth clenched, lips pulled back, and dove into my murky depths, clawing for a hint. My head band heated and vibrated and agony speared through my head. Black dots danced in my eyes as we flew into darkness and then all bets were off as clouds spiralled around us, forming a webbed tunnel. Frigid air streamed around me, stealing my breath. My hands locked around the demon's claws. My stomach hollowed as we spun with the clouds. Round and around and around, they twisted.

Nausea rose in my throat. I swallowed against the urge to vomit before we pulled free of the clouds into near darkness. Shadows hugged the land below my feet. The earth was charred and barren. Broken thatch huts dotted the ground, alongside the blackened bare branches of shrubs. Bones poked through the black dust, half buried in the barren ground. Flames flickered in the distance where a red lava river flowed from jagged mountains.

We dropped towards an enormous castle made from slabs of black stone. Sharpened stone cut into the stonework and lined the walkways like sharks' teeth. Spindly turrets reached towards a blood moon taking up most of the inky sky. The mirrored waters of a moat surrounded the castle, clawing the earth with bloodied veins of crimson.

I moaned out loud as we flew over the walkways filled with black robed figures who stared at us with glowing red eyes. Soul-eaters drifted across the sky, their shadowy cloaks dissipating like smoke around them.

We landed in the courtyard in a swirl of black cloth and sulphur. The demon clutched my wrist and yanked me towards a set of open black steel doors. I tripped over my feet, nearly landing on my knees as he strode up the stairs. He wrenched my arm, keeping me upright. My shoulders screamed, but it was better than going face down on the cold, hard stone.

We strode into a shadowed hallway lit with glowing sconces, giving flickers of light made of nightmares. I would have happily gone back into that tunnel. Would have gladly let the darkness fold over me if it meant I didn't have to see people pinned to the walls with solid metal chains.

Blood stained their dirty skin. Clothing hung from their frail frames, stained with grime, blood and god knew what else. Heavy heads rose to watch as we passed. Some didn't even twitch.

A rat with greasy, mottled fur hissed at us, darted along the wall and disappeared into the inky darkness that pocketed the walls. Groans and wails echoed from the pockets that were more than just thick shadows. Wordless sounds imbued with pain and despair.

I tried to see where Elliot was, but the demon hauled me through another set of doors and into a large antechamber. Roiling clouds swirling overhead hid the ceiling. Pillars lined either side of the room and disappeared into the angry darkness.

Whoever decorated here had a penchant for sconces, because they were on every available surface. The pillars, the walls, the stairs on one side of the room. Shadows would have been preferable to the dancing reflections of the flames because that meant I wouldn't have seen the people packed into the room. 'People' being a relative term.

My legs refused to work. My arm wrenched in its socket when the demon tightened its hold on my upper arm, holding me upright when I failed to get my feet under me. Terror clawed down my spine. Its icy fingers made me freeze and want for better things. My mouth went dry and my heart leapt into my throat as soul-eaters drifted along the walls and lazily passed over my head.

People stared at me, only they weren't people. There was not one trace of civilisation in this room, because nightmares knew no humanity. Faces that were skulls with hollow eyes and permanent grins stood next to tall beings of matt black skin. Twisted horns grew from their heads, the sharp tips gleaming in the firelight. Their eyes were glowing red orbs and white fangs glinted.

Other faces were somewhat human, but their cheeks were sunken, the skin mottled grey. Their hair was matted, greasy clumps between patches of baldness. Their bones poked through thin skin, little more than skeletons. They looked like servants as they carried golden trays from which the other creatures took food or golden metal cups.

A tray clattered to the floor when a black being clawed at one of the walking skeletons and sunk its teeth into the man's neck. Blood sprayed as the black being shredded the man's neck. No one helped, or even moved as the black being ate the man alive. He took another bite and threw the man to the floor, chewing on flesh. The man picked himself up, recovered the tray and the fallen food and continued to serve, shoulders hunched, as though nothing had happened.

I gagged, slapping my palm over my mouth in an attempt to leave the contents of my stomach inside me.

"I find the ones with an ounce of humanity left in their souls make the best servants, and the tastiest food." A female voice echoed through the room.

The beings in the room murmured. Some twittered, nervous and unsure. Beings shifted, shuffling between themselves, whether in fear or anticipation, I didn't know. A woman walked down the stairs, descending from the black haze clinging to the ceiling. At first I could only see her studded, black thigh high leather boots. How she negotiated those stone steps in six inch stilettos, I didn't know. Her dramatic entrance sent a ripple of anticipation through the beings as she revealed herself step by stiletto-clinking. She was pure dominatrix dressed in tight black leather pants and a blood red corset top that made a feature of her slim waist and ample breasts. The brightest thing about her was the white crystal nestled between her ample breasts. It glowed with an inner light that sparkled and danced through the many facets of the domed surface. She was beautiful. Deadly.

Unlike the other beings in this room, this woman was stunning. Her dark hair gleamed in soft waves down to the middle of her back, burning alive with the flickering light thrown from the flames. Her dark eyes sparked with intelligence set in a timelessly beautiful face with prominent brows, cutting cheeks and full, red-stained lips. My skin stretched tight under the relentless weight of her stare as she prowled towards me.

"Bow to your mistress." The demon's voice was gravel and venom as he threw me on the ground at her feet. Dampness soaked into my dress and my palms as I looked up at her. I didn't want to think what the floor was damp from. Certainly nothing I wanted to lend my imagination to.

"It also keeps them somewhat looking like their human manifestation on Earth, but I like the ones who have lost their humanity altogether. They're so...volatile." A smile played on her lips, as though these beings were Kewpie dolls and not creatures from depraved nightmares. Like her beauty, her voice was well-modulated, clear, sultry, and more suited to a movie screen than in a nauseating dungeon. When she turned her stone cold eyes on me, my stomach curled into a tight ball and morphed into lead.

"I... they're..." I felt I should say something, but my words dried like dried leaves in a tornado. The beings watched me as though I was dessert. I wanted to tell them I was all gristle and sinew not even suited for a stew but I didn't think it would matter to them.

Her lips turned up, showing even white teeth, happy with my discomfort. See? Not a bone stuck between them. Maybe she wasn't a monster. Maybe I mistook the mass murder vibe coming off her, but then she opened her mouth, stomping my hopes like bugs. Nasty bitey bugs with huge pinchers and bad attitudes.

She stepped towards me, those killer heels clicking on the stone like nails in my coffin.

"What's this then, little speck?" She traced the golden bans around my forehead. I jerked, only to have the demon wrap his thick claws around the back of my neck to pin me in place.

A scuffle took their attention from me as a demon threw Elliot to the ground. He landed in a sprawled heap. He moaned, pushing himself from the floor as he glared at the stunning beauty. "Get your hands off her, Lilith."

The breath jammed in my lungs. This was Lilith? I'd imagined a toothless old hag. Not someone who looked like a Victoria's Secret model.

Lilith's fingers slid from me, and she sauntered to Elliot. My muscles rusted into flakes, refusing to work with the best of my willpower.

"No." The demon's claws tightened on my neck, but Lilith smiled at me as she put her cherry-coloured talon tipped fingers under Elliot's chin.

Her nails weren't for show. They popped through his skin. He struggled to his knees, breath hissing as she lifted him. "It seems your little girlfriend has jealousy problems."

"You can't take the power from her," Elliot gasped.

"Hmm. I think differently, pet. She used it to get you out of my dungeons and I'll take what I want. All she needs is a little persuasion to hand it over. Then again, I hope she holds off as long as she can. I like to play with my food before I eat."

She placed her hand over Elliot's forehead. His back bowed. His arms stretched back and the tendons popped on his neck. His mouth opened on a soundless scream, but that didn't matter because my scream echoed around the room, bouncing off the cold stone like a million dollar opera house.

She peered at me, her mouth curving into an amused smile. Elliot fell forward, palms slapping the stone, chest working like bellows.

"Get your hands off him!" I screeched.

"So soon? I'm happy to keep playing. It's such fun," Lilith said. She stood in front of me so I was eye level with the red bow of her corset. It looked as perfect as the rest of her, but as beautiful as she was on the outside, she rotted inside. "I don't want to make this a struggle. Release the power and I'll make your death fast. Fight me and I'll hurt him again. The result will be the same either way. The power will be mine and you will cease to exist."

I never would have connected death with a beautiful face, but then again, I knew little. I wanted to curse her. To call her every name I could think of, but when she put the fingers of both hands on the band, all I could do was pant so hard it made me dizzy. My vision hazed at the edges as an electric jolt shot through my temples. The agony turned into something indescribable as drills bored through my skull and made mincemeat of my brain.

Cold, slimy energy burrowed deep down inside me, into the marrow of my soul. My consciousness narrowed to the steel tipped energy swords slicing me apart, imbued with Lilith's energy.

She carved into me, traces of her dark energy burning wherever she touched. She came up against the fragments in my mind, leaping between them as she tried to seal the power embedded into them. I cringed as she left traces of her essence in all parts of my mind. She burned where she touched, leaving blackened scars where she shredded.

Words sounded on the outskirts of my screams, their soothing, serpentine texture like a balm against Lilith's white-hot carnage. The words melted into me, anaesthetising the burn, allowing me a moment of clarity.

Elliot spoke those words. I recognised the soft timbre of his voice. The words slid from his tongue in supple, sinuous tones, clearing a path to that deepest part of me that shone with glowing white. Energy, vast and great, called for me with an urge too powerful to deny. I tumbled into the shimmery river. White burst around me, blinding me, filling me. Becoming me.

My consciousness exploded, the white soaking every dark corner and crevice of my soul. Power streamed through me hard and fast, powering through my veins, stuffing my mind and turning me into something *more*. Something that considered Lilith's energy an abomination. That needed to be culled.

I jerked, chest expanding, heart bursting as a bomb went off inside me. Power shot through me in a flash of white. I was thrown from the river of white, Lilith's talons wilting like blades of grass. I burst from my body as a shock wave cracked from my skin. I collapsed onto my back, the breath knocked out of me.

I tried to suck in air, but my lungs worked against me. I blinked the black from my vision to see soul-eaters crushed against the upper walls. Beings strewn across the floor, bodies on bodies, hands stretching, arms reaching, formed a writhing living carpet. My neck free from the clasp of demon claws.

Elliot scrambled to his knees, eyes wild, calling for me. I couldn't hear him through the white noise in my ears. I reached for him, muscles mired in mud. He grabbed my wild swing, his hand clasping mine.

He rose on rubbery legs, his steady strength surprising me as he tugged me to my feet. Fingers clenched in mine, he hauled me through the room, jumping across sprawled limbs and bodies and into the deepest shadow.

"Stop them!" Lilith's screech followed us into the doorway and the corridor beyond.

We bolted into the darkness.

Chapter Twelve

Elliot's fingers firmed around mine as we ran the length of the dim corridor. High-pitched screeches reverberated around us and shadows chased my heels. I glanced over my shoulder and stumbled because I should have been concentrating on where I put my feet and also because soul-eaters burst from the darkness behind us.

"This way," Elliot rasped.

His hold firmed on my hand as he propelled me around a sharp bend and into another corridor made from rough, grey brick. Flames lined the walls. Emaciated beings dressed in rags or nothing at all hung like macabre wall art. It was hard to tell if they were dead or unconscious, their bones poking out from under grey, loose skin. Screeches followed us as we pounded over damp, uneven stones. This place was terrifying.

Elliot stopped at a closed door and rammed it open with his shoulder. We stumbled into an open room before he slammed a thick plank across the closed door. The stench of rotting skin, faeces and vomit hit me in the face. I wretched, my stomach cramping. Hot bile rose up my throat and I clamped my hand over my mouth trying miserably to push it back down. I shook. Trembled. Fell apart and a groan ripped up my throat when I saw where we were.

"Don't look, Cassie. They can get out whenever they want," Elliot said, urging me through the room.

It didn't look like they could. Not when they were strapped to tables, pinned by steel spikes, had limbs severed, blood trickling from open wounds, intestines spread across the floor. No matter how the shrieks and wails built up on the other side of the door, my muscles tightened until my joints locked solid and I could move no further.

Elliot gripped my face between his warm palms. "Look at me, Cassie."

I fought to bring my gaze to his, and failed, dropping to the floor instead where the intestines mixed with faeces and god knew whatever else. A rat squeaked and ran off with a severed finger in its mouth.

"They do this to themselves. They torture themselves. They're murderers. Rapists. The worst of humanity. They're here because their souls are dark, and this is what dark souls do to themselves. If they ask for forgiveness for their deeds, find the light in their souls, then they will cross into the next dimension where their vibrations will resonate," Elliot whispered, his voice hard and tense, as he reached down to lift me from the filthy floor.

I licked dry lips. "How do you know?"

This could be Lilith's play room. The place she came to for funsies. I knew she did because she'd left a little piece of herself inside me. I'd touched her soul and it had left its mark.

"Because this is what we try and save humanity from when we incarnate. We keep souls in the light, where they can grow and love. We try to keep them from doing this to themselves," Elliot said.

The door creaked. The wails hit like a category five tornado, forcing me backwards. The tortured beings in the room whimpered and moaned. It was hard to see that people would do this to themselves, but Elliot hadn't taken his eyes or his hands off me. A muscle ticked at his temple and his mouth pressed into a hard line.

He wouldn't lie to me. I trusted him with every part of my soul, even if I didn't understand why something like this would happen.

I gave him a sharp nod. He dipped his lips to mine, took my hand and led me to the opposite side of the room where stairs, carved into the wall, led upwards. I kept my gaze on Elliot's back, putting my feet where he put his, breathing through my mouth and trying to ignore the wasps buzzing in my stomach.

We rushed across a stone tiled landing. Elliot kicked in a closed wooden door and we clambered through as soul-eaters broke through the door on the ground floor. They flew towards us, shrieking black shadows, claws extended, mouths yawning open as the tortured ones below screamed.

Elliot pulled me through and slammed the door behind us. My heart bashed my sternum, threatening to shatter my bones to ram out of my body. The air here was cloying. Frigid. The red velvet floor and wooden panelled walls surrounding me did little to calm me.

The door thumped. The wailing created a screaming cacophony as the wood strained. Elliot tested the next door in the hallway, but his best effort failed to open it. We ran to the next, but it was cemented shut as well. The corridor was a dead end, with nothing but a full length painting of Lilith hanging on the panelling. She peered down at us, her expression haughty and cold. Whoever had painted it had captured her perfectly.

The hallway door splintered. Shards shattered as a soul-eater punched through the wood and extended its claws towards us. Elliot grabbed my arm, hauling me along the corridor and shoving me against Lilith's painting. He wrapped himself around my body, pressing his chest against mine, elbows pinning either side of my head, thighs braced on the outside of mine.

He was going to use himself as a barrier, protecting me from the soul-eaters, by using the only thing he had - himself - as the last obstacle. I looked into his eyes, into those mossy depths that were the last thing I wanted to see before the soul-eaters took me to Lilith and she killed me for the power.

The painting at my back fell away, hands gripped my shoulders and hauled me backwards. A dark figure slammed the painting against the wall, shutting out the light from the corridor and leaving us in darkness.

"This way. Quickly," a male voice said.

Elliot was wrenched from my grip and I lost all sense of direction as a tall, strong man picked me up and threw me over his shoulders. We ran through the inky darkness. I kicked and squirmed, but he clamped his arm about my thighs, holding me tight.

"I mean you no harm," he said, but I knew better.

He could be a soul who was so screwed up he was acting out, or he could be pretending to be my friend to take me to Lilith.

"Elliot!" I screamed, or I tried to because my gut slammed into his thick shoulder and all the breath left my lungs. No matter how hard I tried sucking it back in, my body wasn't having any of that.

I was sure black dots edged my vision, but it was too hard to tell when we ran through impenetrable darkness. Footfalls scuffed the floor. Heavy breaths sounded over the pounding of blood in my ears.

We cut a sharp corner and through another door. It slammed shut behind us, the snick loud as it closed sharp and final. We clambered down stairs, shoes clattering on stone that echoed somewhere far above and below before someone's hand slapped another door open. We passed through the doorway into a dimly lit corridor. I still couldn't see because my hair hung in my face and the black leather pants and heavy boots told me nothing of the man carrying me.

We twisted through an endless run of corridors, the stone beneath his feet unrelenting as his shoulder ramming my midsection. My head throbbed, and filled with blood. It was too hard to hold on to his shirt, my fingers numb and weakening.

Lilith would not end me. I was going to perish by being hauled around like a sack of potatoes. Hinges squeaked, and we stepped into another room. Crimson carpet filled my vision before the man pulled me off his shoulder and set me on my feet.

My feet sucked the blood that had pooled in my head, angry at being denied blood flow. I swayed, knees week, desperately trying to clear my vision through a thousand blinks. Hands steadied me, keeping me upright while I rode the wave of nausea churning up my throat.

"I'm sorry, Amirel," a deep voice said. "We had to move as quickly as possible."

I gulped in deep breaths. His words slide inside my skull. I started at him while I tried to make sense of his words. *Sorry? He knew my name?*

Familiar arms wrapped around me. Elliot crushed me against him, dipping his face against my neck and breathing me in. "Are you all right, Cassie?"

I sunk my fingers into Elliot's shirt, shuddering and hugging him as tightly as he held me. "I am now."

I clenched my eyes hard, willing myself somewhere else, but when I opened my eyes to see if my imagination had somehow replaced reality, it was to see a man peering at me above Elliot's shoulder.

His dark brown hair was a mess on top of his head, the long strands threatening to drop over his eyes. A bushy beard hid half his long face. He was head and shoulders taller than Elliot, and broad. My bruised stomach attested to the hard-packed muscles in them; more bear than man. He wore tight, black breeches tucked into thick boots, and a black shirt over which he wore a black leather vest. It was no wonder I failed to see him in the darkness. Despite his size, he blended into the shadows like he was born in them.

"Why do you use Amirel's incarnate name, Siel?" A woman, also dressed all in black, stepped forward. A frown pulled her otherwise smooth brow beneath which startling hazel eyes watched me in concern. Her skin was a deep tan. She'd tied her long dark hair into a long ponytail that ended halfway down her back. Her full rosebud pink lips were pursed.

How did she know Elliot? Who the hell were these people? "Who are you?"

The woman's mouth fell open. Her gaze swung from me to Elliot, her brows forming a line between their perfectly sleek arches. "You don't recognise me?"

She looked at me as though I should know her and yet the familiar wall of nothing hit me. These holes in my mind were irritating me. I winced as a headache beat drums behind my eyes.

"No, I don't recognise you." I didn't trust her or the man either, and I wondered how Lilith let two normal looking people knock about her castle. "Why are you here? Why do you look normal?"

"They're not tortured souls, Cassie. They're Light-Stream workers." Elliot clapped his hand on the big guy's shoulder. "Thank you for coming for us, Ezra. For a moment there..."

"Say no more." Ezra shook Elliot's hand off to wrap his tree trunk arms around Elliot in a grip so forceful, Elliot lost his breath in a whoosh. "There was no way we would let those abominations take you from us."

Elliot tapped Ezra's bulging bicep. The big man released him, and then Elliot crossed to the woman and hugged her. My skin itched with perspiration. Elliot knew these people?

"Thank you, Avril. You put yourselves in danger for us and I'll be grateful forever," Elliot said.

She smiled, accepting Elliot's hug before he stepped back to me. I moulded myself to Elliot's side. Elliot wrapped his arm around my waist, pinning me against him and helping to keep the urge not to claw her to a manageable level.

"Cassie, these are Ezra and Avril. They're not in our soul group, but they are here to help us," Elliot said.

"Cassie?" Avril asked, tilting her head, her brow furrowed. "I wasn't hearing things when you called her that name before?"

Elliot's grip around my waist tightened, as he pushed his breath out in a gush. "This will... take some explaining."

"We're safe here, Siel. We've warded this room. Lilith can't detect us here. Sit down and rest with us. There is much to talk about," Ezra said.

We were in a room that was more lavish bordello than bedroom. Restful was not a word I would use to describe a room in a crimson and red patterned wallpaper. The firelight picked out the golden thread that highlighted the pattern.

The massive bed was the most impressive piece of furniture in the room. The couches, chairs and tables were secondary to its size. A canopy of black velvet draped over four intricately carved posts. Black and gold cushions took up half of the bed, but the mattress looked soft and it took most of my willpower not to curl up in the middle of them.

Floor to ceiling windows opened to a balcony overlooking the landscape stretching far below. Jagged mountains clawed the crimson sky along the horizon. Rivers of molten lava trailed down the sides of the mountains and into the sweeping dead valley below, slashing the barren spread of rocks and black dirt with streaks of red and oranges. It was stark, horrifying and yet strangely beautiful and suddenly I was exhausted.

Elliot sat me in one of the four chairs and took one next to mine. Ezra and Avril sat in the chairs opposite after placing a tray of fruit and a jug of water on the table. I hadn't realised how thirsty I was until I saw the water.

Avril poured two glasses and handed one to me and the other to Elliot. I shoved the strange jealousy aside and gave her a small smile before chugging the water. It was cool in my parched throat and I hated knowing she'd anticipated my need.

"We came here as soon as Ruhiel sent word of a portal breach and your presences detected in Hellioth," Ezra said.

Elliot stiffened. He placed his empty cup on the table. "Did you get Thomas and Ben out?"

Avril shook her head and clutched her hands in her lap. "They're still locked in the dungeons. We had plans to break you all out before a portal opened for you. When that happened, Lilith multiplied the guards and strengthened the barriers between dimensions. We haven't been able to contact Ruhiel, or to cross dimensions."

"They're all blocked. Lilith used the soul-eaters to circumvent the doorways. They captured us and brought us here," Elliot said.

I didn't miss the look of confusion on both Ezra's and Avril's faces. "Soul-eaters?" Avril asked.

"They're the horrible, nightmarish creatures chasing us," I said.

Ezra's eyes flared, and he reeled back in his seat. "We had no name for them. We couldn't detect their origin."

"Soul-eaters were made. They don't belong to any dimension, but cross dimensions when no one else can," Elliot said.

Ezra and Avril shared a look that was a cross between stark horror and morbid sickness.

"Impossible," Avril whispered.

"I wish it was, but they are very much real, and created to consume souls," Elliot said.

"Are they the reason the portals are locked?" Ezra said, his hands clenching around the arm-rests.

"That would be because of me," I said.

Avril tilted her head, a frown still creasing her forehead. "How can it be your fault, Amirel?"

Weight pressed on my shoulders, as heavy and oppressive as the band still around my head. This whole situation was my fault. Dimensions. Countless lives. All at risk. Because of me. The air in the room was stifling, and I couldn't breathe through the steel strap that forever tightened around my chest.

Elliot squeezed my hand and the pressure eased enough for me to draw breath. Elliot could explain, but this was my mess. It needed to come from me, and if Elliot trusted them, then I should too. They should know the danger they'd put themselves in to save me.

I ignored the jackhammers inside my skull, drew a breath and forced the words out. "With his dying breath, Hadriel gave me his power. I don't know why. It doesn't matter what his reasons were, but Lilith wants it. She brought me here to take it and now you're all in danger. She won't stop until she has it and if you try to stop her, she'll kill you too. She won't let anything stand in her way. Not you. Not Elliot. Not even my death."

The jackhammers turned into drills. Freezing cold drills that bored into my skull. I cried out, flaring my hands over the band on my forehead. It vibrated, burning hot enough to sear my skin. The energy was dark. Evil. Familiar.

Lilith.

Her phantom energy pierced through me, icing me from the inside out.

"Cassie. What is it? What's happening?" Elliot said.

Elliot wavered through my watery vision. I'd put him through so much worry. It poured off him, tangling with the darkness invading my head. I couldn't speak; couldn't utter a syllable. The water I'd drunk churned in my gut with the sheer intention of coming back up.

Lilith had entered my head, and I couldn't get her out.

Chapter Thirteen

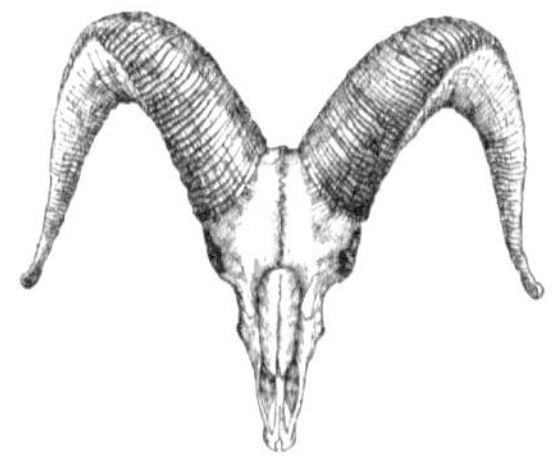

"Cassie, come back to me." Elliot's gravelly voice pushed the torment to the outskirts of my mind.

I blinked open rusted shut eyelids to find Elliot kneeling in front of me, stroking his fingers through my hair. I concentrated on his soothing touches, letting them ground me. His brows drew together, his gaze riveted on me.

Ezra and Avril stood behind him. Avril wrung her hands while Ezra's frown furrowed his brow. I guessed I scared them with my mind disappearing act. Truth be told, I scared myself too.

Elliot's breath whooshed out when he weighed my gaze on him. "Thank god. You're back."

"Want to tell us what just happened?" Ezra said, folding his tree trunk arms across his massive chest.

I sank against the backrest of the chair, letting my limbs and muscles ooze into the cushioning. "It's Lilith."

I tilted on the precipice of a slippery slope, and there was only one way to go. The pain in my head was stronger. Sharper. I'd lost time - lost *myself* - and I wouldn't ask how long Elliot had been trying to get me back to my senses.

I rubbed my temples, although it did nothing to soothe the throbbing behind my eyes. I'd give anything for an aspirin, but Hellioth was big on torture. No pain meds to be found anywhere here. "I can still feel her digging with her daggers in my brain."

"Residual energy," Avril muttered.

I squinted at her. I would go insane long before my mind fractured if I couldn't get Lilith out. "How do I stop it?"

"The only way for you to be stronger than Lilith and to manage Hadriel's power is to culminate your lifetimes past, present - and future," Elliot said, his voice now more than gravel.

Going by Ezra's disbelieving gasp, that wasn't a good thing. Way to go, backing me up with all that confidence. My personal cheerleading team was nothing if I couldn't get to my akashic records in this dimension. It wasn't exactly a place for a library of knowledge to manifest. The souls here were tortured, not trying to expand their minds.

"I can't do that without my life books," I said. "Unless we can hijack a soul-eater, there's no getting back to the library."

Avril paced, biting off a hangnail. "There may be a way."

While the words piqued my interest, I didn't appreciate the tone that made it sound like I may soon attend my own funeral. "I'll do anything to get Lilith out of my head."

"What are you thinking about, Avril?" Elliot said.

"The Heart Stone," Avril said.

"That's...no..." Elliot shook his head, and a tuft of hair fell into his eyes. He swiped it back with a quick jerk.

Forget Avril's tone. I didn't like this whole conversation.

Elliot drew my hand into his. A fine tremor worked through his fingers, travelling all the way to my soft-centre. The words 'why me' almost left my lips, but I caught them in time. There was no answer to that question, and no excuse to feel sorry for myself. This situation was nobody's fault and Ezra and Avril were trying to help before I collapsed every dimension and annihilated everyone in it.

As though I'd summoned it, a wave of energy surged. It crashed through me, bringing with it images of people, places and fragmented scenes I had no hope of understanding. Celestial beings, human faces, non-human faces flashed through my mind. A torrent of white energy gushed with the force of a geyser. Unmitigated power pounded through me, uncontrolled and violent, before a circle of hands clasped together around the jet of energy. Some were human hands, some clawed, and others made from pure light.

My bones locked as electricity burned through them. Power coursed through me, making petrified wood of my body. Serpentine words slid through my mind, too slippery to understand, but the power reduced from its thunderous, uncontrolled spew of energy to a controlled streamlined force. The jagged edges smoothed as the hands moved it with deliberate movements.

White light flashed, disappeared, and I floated in darkness. Someone tapped my cheek, annoying me. I went to push them away with a hand that was more brick than flesh.

"Cassie! Come back to me!" Elliot's urgent tone speared through the darkness, wrapping me up and drawing me out.

Elliot hovered above me, brows drawn, mossy eyes darkly focussed on me. His fingers on my cheek trembled. "Are you back with me, Cassie?"

A glance told me I was in the overstated, yet luxurious, bed on a sea of black silk with Elliot stretched out next to me. His body heat warmed me from my shoulders to my toes as every inch of his muscular body pressed against me. I dragged his masculine spice into my lungs, using his familiar scent to centre me.

"How..?" I asked. How had I ended up in the bed when I'd been sitting in the chair?

"You blacked out again, Cassie," Elliot said, his full lips turned down as he stroked my hair, holding me like I might shatter into a million pieces. I already was.

We were the only two in the room. "Where are Ezra and Avril?"

"They're making sure the area is clear," Elliot said.

I gripped the hand, trailing over my jaw. I'd lost time again. Suddenly I didn't want to think about blacking out. About power fracturing me apart. About my soul being the worm on the hook. About seeing images I had no words for. I didn't want to think about any of that.

This may be the last time we could be together. There was no telling what was going to happen from one moment to the next, and I would not waste a precious second.

"I just want to feel you, Elliot," I said. "Can you make it all go away? For a few minutes?" My vision wavered as tears built in my eyes.

His eyes darkened, catching me in a maelstrom of concern and heat. I didn't want him to pity me. Or not touch me because he thought I'd break. I captured his nape with my hand, brought him down to me, pressed his lips on mine and demanded he kiss me.

He needed no encouragement. His hand slid under my head, rolled on top of me, and my body sank into the impossibly soft mattress with his weight. His moan vibrated in my mouth, making my belly roll and my core throb before his tongue swept into my mouth, and sparks erupted through my body.

I rubbed my thigh along his hips and he clutched me tighter. I clung to him, using his body to anchor myself to this moment

I never wanted to end. I was raw. Desperate. His arms were the only place I felt protected.

If I were honest, I was terrified; breaking down in more ways than fracturing apart with this power.

"We'll think of a way to get us through, Cassie," Elliot whispered.

I held him above me, our breathing mingling. I wanted to say what if we didn't? What if these were our last moments? But I didn't want to speak them out loud. I drew his shirt from his pants and over his head, kissing his shoulder, his pecs, any part of him I could find with my mouth, and simply agreed with him. In this moment, I didn't want to think any other way. "Yes. We will."

His breath stuttered before he drew my dress over my head. He unclasped my bra and then his hot mouth was on my breast, sucking my beaded nipple into his mouth. He settled between my parted thighs, nestling his hardness where I ached. I tilted my hips, needing the friction and the pressure to ease the ache.

Elliot massaged my other breast while he suckled. He kissed a path between them, closing his mouth over my other breast and swirling my hardened nub with his tongue. His groan sparked through me, tightening the coil that already wound tight in my belly. "I want you so badly."

"I want you too, Elliot," I gasped.

My body hummed with excitement at his wet lips and the heat radiating from his eyes. His hands curved on my waist as he drew himself down my body, to kneel between my thighs. My core clenched as his fingers brushed my belly, sliding his fingers beneath my underwear and sliding them off my legs.

"I don't think you understand the length I'll go to, to protect you." Elliot's voice was low. A solemn vow made to me. My fingers sunk into his hair as I gazed at him. The weight of his words wrapped around me. They were the same words I say back to him in a heartbeat. There was nothing I wouldn't do for him. He was mine. He was *everything.*

He leaned down to kiss me, his lips crashing against mine. He slid his tongue inside my mouth, catching my doubts with each deep sweep. I moaned into his mouth, needing every bit of himself that he'd give me. He drugged me with his lips and tongue, and melted my body with each caress and squeeze of his hands.

I wanted more than just this time; much more than this once that could be our last time together.

Elliot drew his pants off, and then he was between my parted thighs. His hard, hot length slid through my folds in the most exquisite way. I was wet, ready and waiting for him. I ground myself against him, clit throbbing, groaning when a frisson of sparks rushed through me as he settled his weight over my lower body.

"Please, Elliot. Please." My mouth watered as he tilted his hips, gliding through my wetness. I was so sensitive that I cried out, my nerves on fire. My desire to have him inside me built to overflowing.

"You never have to wait for me," Elliot groaned.

I burned from the inside out as he notched the tip of himself to my entrance then slid inside my willing body, locking my gaze with his until he'd seated every glorious inch of himself inside me to the hilt. So full. So complete. My back arched, and I cried out at his welcome invasion, fingers clawing his arms, mouth falling open on a breathless moan.

His fingers tangled in my hair as he titled my head back and kissed me. My hands shook as I buried them in his hair, wrapping him in my arms around his neck, his shoulders, his waist. I opened my legs, cradling him between my thighs. He crushed his pelvis against mine, putting pressure on my clit. The muscles in my channel squeezed him, searing me with heat. He throbbed inside me, his shaft pulsing, and we both groaned.

He dragged himself out of me before slamming back. His pelvis rubbed my clit, liquefying my body, each thrust exquisite torture. He filled me thoroughly. Deeply. Giving his whole self to me, completing me in a way that no one else ever could. The sounds of his gravelly moans filled my ears. Every thrust hit the deepest part of me. His pelvis hit mine, rubbing and pounding against the most intimate parts of my body. I tilted my hips, accepting each thrust, wanting more. Always wanting more.

His body covered mine, from hips to shoulders. He kissed me, thrusting into my mouth with his tongue the way he thrust into my core. His perspiration mingled with mine; his body locked with mine. Two halves coming together as a whole.

My eyelids closed, white power washing the darkness away. Impressions of faces formed from within the power. Faces I felt I should know but couldn't define. They spun around me, teasing me with meaning just out of my reach. Metaphorical hands extended towards me and as I strained for them licking flames of power cut me off from them. My climax broke through me, hurtling me away from the power and the faces as exquisite pleasure exploded through me.

Elliot pulsed inside me. His body tensed, his fingers firmed in my hair, and his moan washed around me, mixing with my pleasure-filled scream as I shattered into a thousand pieces. I spiralled with my climax to that place where we met on a soul level. His energy brushed against mine, welcome, calming.

I floated back, sated. Elliot rolled me to my side, still inside me, holding me tenderly, kissing me, petting me, looking at me as though committing me to memory. As though he didn't believe that we would win.

As though this was the last time we would make love and this was the last time he'd hold me in his arms.

Chapter Fourteen

Elliot helped me into jeans and a t-shirt he'd manifested before dressing himself with the familiar style of his clothing. I couldn't help but feel he was covering more than his body. He was also armouring himself against the possibility that we weren't getting out of here in one piece.

"Siel. Amirel!" Ezra hissed from behind the room's locked door.

Elliot crossed to the door and let him and Avril in.

Ezra's gaze tracked between us. "If we hope to make it to the temple, we have to leave now," he said.

"Lilith is searching the castle for you. The passageways on this side of the castle are not so bad, but it's only a matter of time before they come searching here," Avril said, her soft eyes landing on me. I recognised the apology in them and braced myself because it wouldn't make hearing them any easier. "It doesn't give us a lot of time or space to prepare."

I was right. Her words were lead bullets, and I held a red bulls-eye over my stomach. My blood turned to sleet when Elliot placed his hands in mine. "Whatever happens to me, go with Ezra and Avril..."

He was preparing to sacrifice himself for me. "No!" The word punched from my mouth. An instant denial. "That will not happen, Elliot."

I would not let that happen. I was the person Lilith was after. I'd fractured apart. If anyone had the better chance of stopping her, it was him.

Elliot's fingers carded in my hair. "Go with Ezra and Avril. Do whatever you can to protect the power. It cannot fall into Lilith's hands."

His words slammed into my chest like fast punches, knocking the breath right out of me.

"Please, Cassie. This is the only way. You know this," he whispered. His lips found mine, and I kissed him back desperately, as though I hadn't made love with him minutes before.

"It doesn't make it right," I said.

"None of this is right, but we have to deal with the play. You are my everything, Cassie. Forget everything else, but remember that," Elliot said.

Avril shifted her weight. Tension was a live wire radiating from her body. We weren't the only people without risk. I firmed my shoulders and ignored the endless hole in the pit of my stomach. I squeezed Elliot's hands. "Okay. Let's do what needs to be done."

It wasn't as though any of us had a choice.

Ezra peered around the door, his huge frame blocking most of it. He turned his shaggy head over his shoulder. "Clear."

I fought the metaphorical chains attached to lead balls around my feet and followed Ezra down the corridor styled in the same bad-bordello style as the bedroom, while Avril followed behind us. A crimson carpet runner lay over floorboards. Panelled wooden walls of dark wood made up the bottom half of the walls. Black and silver wallpaper made from an endless pattern of large flowers took the top half.

Mounted on the wall, paintings depicting images of tortured charred bodies and demons eating the flesh of screaming humans confronted me. In all the paintings stood a demon with four arms and deep red skin. Her fingers flowed into long, black claws that could be described as elegant. A hock jointed leg supported muscular legs. The three claws of her feet dug into the charcoal soil. Her tail whipped behind her, topped with a lethal triangular blade. The long white hair whipped around her shoulders as she overlooked the carnage.

In some paintings, blood coated her lips and chin while she ate people alive. In others, she used her claws as spears. Each image was more depraved than the last. I forced my eyes from the horrifying scenes.

"We have to use the outside stairs to get to the dungeons," Avril whispered behind us. "They'll be the safest way down."

Outside stairs? I stopped at her words and tripped over my feet. Elliot steadied me. I'd seen the view from the bedroom and we were at least twenty stories high.

"We have to get Thomas and Ben out of the dungeons. We need them for the Heart Stone," Elliot said.

I was regretting not having the state of mind to ask what the Heart Stone actually was and how it was going to help. I opened my mouth to do just that, when Ezra dashed around a corner, taking us into a short corridor with a black door at the end.

He twisted the large brass doorknob and threw the door open. I stumbled backwards, every muscle in my body screaming at me to get back to safety. An automatic response to the scene on the other side of the door.

Instead of a room, or another corridor, this door opened to the landscape spread far below, and nothing else. No ledge with a sturdy barrier. No tricky little window for thrill seekers that was really an optical illusion. No pane of protective glass.

"Hurry. This way," Ezra stepped out into the open air and — disappeared.

The breath petrified in my lungs. "Where?"

"It's okay. Concentrate on your feet and you'll be fine," Elliot said.

I clung to Elliot's hand as he urged me to the door from hell to see Ezra on a narrow set of steps cut into the stone wall of the outside of the castle. He balanced on the side closest to the wall, his huge body in danger of toppling over.

My survival instincts knocked into overdrive. "You want me to go out there?"

Out there was the seed of nightmares. The stone steps were barely wide enough for my feet. Half of Ezra's feet went over the width. There was no handrail either. Only rectangular slabs of stone stabbed into the brickwork that went longer than I could see. The 'stairs' twisted around the bend of the wall and out of sight.

"I'll help," Ezra said.

"I'll be behind you all the way," Elliot said.

Avril's sharp inhale preceded the soft click of the door closing behind us. She walked quickly over to us, her eyes wide and dark. "Demons are coming. We need to move. Quickly."

It was the stairs or the demons. At least with the stairs I had a slight chance of survival. I wrapped my smaller hand in Ezra's and stepped onto the first stone slab.

I pushed my back against the wall, perspiration beading on my forehead. I was outside, a long, *long* way above the ground. If I fell, I wondered if I would die here. Was that even possible? People here were tortured over and over. They were hurt enough to die, and yet the demon had taken a chunk out of the man before and he'd got back on his feet, with his neck healed. Rivers of lava glowed on the horizon and were those soul-eaters flying in the distance?

Elliot's fingers curled around my shoulders, centring me. I drew in a deep breath. If I didn't pull myself together, it wasn't only me who was going to be caught. I could do this.

I focussed on my feet, moved to the next step, and then the next. I made the mistake of looking between the slabs, to the crimson moat way, *waaayyy* below. My legs locked, and I flattened my back on the wall, palms splayed either side of me. If I could grow suction cups on my fingers, I'd happily become a new breed of human. The stone prickled my back, squashing the bead of sweat trickling down my spine as I clenched my eyes closed.

Forget about the ground. Forget about the soul-eaters flying in the distance. Forget about everything except taking that next step. My head was a blank mess. I should take advantage of that nothingness between my ears and forget about the terror that filled my veins, but that kind of baggage stuck to the inside of my skull like mud.

"You're doing great, Amirel," Ezra said.

"How do...do you know us? Know Elliot?" I asked as I followed Ezra step after laborious step. If I concentrated on something else, it would take my mind off the possibility of landing on the hard ground below. Unlike the man who had his neck eaten, I didn't know if I'd regenerate here.

"Although we are not in the same soul group, we are all Light-Stream workers, dedicated to saving humanity from misuse of the power gifted to humanity from beyond the veil," Ezra said. "We've incarnated a few times and worked together to help humanity when the time has called for it."

"We fought in the Egyptian army in eastern Mediterranean with the Hittites and Mitanians when they misused the power of Ra," Avril said.

"And again in the Punic Wars when we were Roman generals fighting Carthage," Ezra said.

"Scipio Africanus only defeated Hannibal because he stole the flaming sword from Adam after he was banished. Who would have thought temples would have been built in the Petra caves and the sword smuggled out. That was tricky to get a hold of," Avril said, her feet tapping the steps as we descended.

A tingle of familiarity flew through me, but then it was lost in the mire in my skull. "You mean Elliot incarnated with you in those times?"

"You too, Amirel," Ezra said. "In fact, you rose to become a general in the Roman army and took the sword from Scipio yourself."

"I..." I wanted to say that I remembered. That I was the culmination of these lives I was meant to have lived. It sounded fantastical. Almost too hard to believe, and if I weren't descending the stone steps on a castle clearly not of Earth, I would have written it off as complete fiction.

The headband vibrated, and a throb broke behind my eyes when I tried to remember. It was no use. I was splintering apart, the fractured breaking down into smaller parts that would never fit back together again. Anything I was before I woke in that white room with Ibn caring for me was gone as though it had never happened.

My foot slipped. Elliot gripped my bicep and prevented me from falling into the crimson moat that was now just below my feet. Dark shapes swam beneath the viscous liquid and I glimpsed a black angular face with sharp white teeth before it disappeared under the surface.

I pulled my eyes off the whatever-the-hell that was swimming in the moat and peered up in the direction we'd descended from past Elliot's shoulder. The steps rose far above me. Various windows and doors were carved in the castle's walls and I was surprised to see ours weren't the only outer steps on the walls. We'd climbed down faster than I thought while I'd tried to remember the parts of me I'd forgotten.

"Through here," Ezra said.

The steps led to a notched door set into the stone. The hinges squealed as he opened the door. I followed Ezra into the darkness, grateful to be off the steps and the open and yet terrified to be back in another dank tunnel with thin flames for lighting.

Elliot's body heat wrapped around me from behind as he followed us in. Thick darkness enveloped us when Avril closed the door.

Elliot put his finger to his lips when I was about to ask where we were. The stale smell of urine and fear should have told me we were close to the dungeons. Elliot took my hand and we followed Ezra along the corridor. Stone bricks arched around us, and the uneven cobblestones underfoot were damp with god-knew-what. Going by the increasing stench, it'd been a long time since this tunnel, or anything attached to it, had been cleaned.

The floor sloped downwards and grew dank. My breath frosted in the air, and the taste of hopelessness coated my tongue. Closed doors were set into the walls and rusted shut. Chains clattered behind some, while silence reigned behind others. I shuddered to think of whoever or whatever was in there.

Elliot's jaw was set in a firm line, the muscle working his temple as he walked with purpose. My stomach rolled with a barrel of rocks thinking that he'd been stuck down here before I'd called a portal for him. What had he been subjected to? Had he been chained to a wall? Or eaten alive, only to regenerate?

I swallowed down the hot bile that rose in my throat. One day I would ask him. Or perhaps it was better I never did. Nobody would want to relive memories of their time here.

I hated to think he'd been stuck here with tortured souls. Appalled that such a place existed. How were any of them meant to find any light in a place like this?

I almost ran into Ezra's back when he stopped at a junction. Voices echoed softly down the corridor, followed by feet scuffing stone and the sound of chains clanking. I peered around his shoulder to see a room that had been carved out of stone, as though the room was a cave instead of built from the rough stones of the castle.

Several sets of bars were set into alcoves, the depth of which I couldn't make out through the darkness beyond the bars. Shadows shifted in some of them. A set of hairy hands clutched around bars disappeared, a large body shuffling in the shadows.

In the centre of the room was a raised dais, rising from the floor that looked as though someone had carved it with the same chisel as the walls. My blood ran cold, seeing instruments stained with rust thrown on the top. There was no mistaking what the studded ball on a chain, nor the open bear trap, or the bat with jagged nails were used for. The instruments of torture were piled in a heap and I wasn't stupid enough to think that was rust on them either.

Or to think they weren't used.

A long, suffering sigh brought my attention to the centre alcove. Two men came to the front of their cell, both so achingly familiar, yet their identities were out of reach. My attention focussed on the man leaving to slide his arms through the bars to rest on a horizontal bar that divided them in half. His face merged from the shadows. His brown hair was tousled and thick with grime. His eyes slid closed when he rested his head against the bars, but not before I noticed their striking colour green. I frowned, the familiar sensation niggling at the back of my mind, and peered at Elliot.

He watched me, his mouth set in a grim line, his face so similar to the man in the cell. So similar they could be related.

I gasped, the small sound I made echoed throughout the chamber. The man in the cell's face lifted, his eyes flashing open.

I stepped towards him, my feet hesitating. I was safe with Elliot, but with this man...I didn't feel safe. Not at all. I hoped that this wasn't the man we were here to rescue, because my stomach rolled in that way that pounded on my internal alert button.

Ezra stepped forward into the cavern and the sirens blared inside my head. The man who looked like Elliot straightened. "Ezra!"

Ezra picked up a weapon with the ball and spikes. "Ben. Thomas. Glad to see you're still standing. We're here to get you out."

Chapter Fifteen

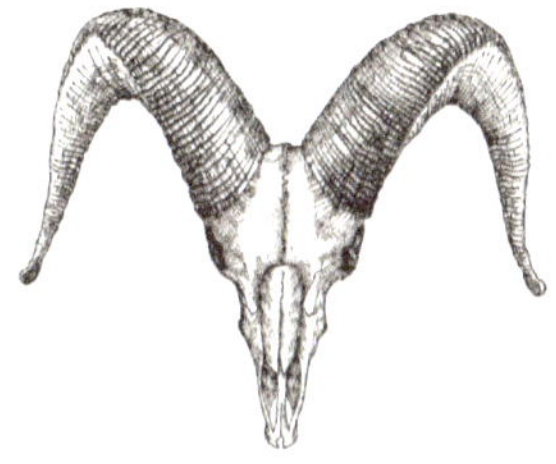

Ezra hit the lock, shattering it after several hits. The lock dropped to the ground with a clank and Ben and Thomas pushed the door open. The hinges scraped and then they were out. Their clothing was filthy, as were their hair and skin. Bruises marred their forearms, necks and faces, and probably were all over their body in places I couldn't see. The man resembling Elliot favoured his left leg. There was a tear in his pants, the edges stained with blood and filth. I stiffened, looking at how dirty the wound was. That would lead to sepsis if someone didn't disinfect it soon. I frowned, wondering how I knew that and why I should care about a man who sent chills up my spine.

"Thank god, you're here," the man I didn't know said. "When you stepped through that portal, there was no way of telling where you ended up. How did a portal open up anyway? And why did it just take you?"

Elliot stepped towards them, hugging one and then the other. "Ben. Thomas." He clapped the man who looked like him on the back. "Cassie summoned me. She opened the portal."

Thomas' brows drew tight. "Cassie? We're going by our last incarnate names?"

"For now." Elliot held his hand out to me, wanting me to leave my safe place.

"Come on, Cassie. It's safe here for now," Avril said. She grasped my hand, but I couldn't make my legs work to take me into the chamber. I couldn't stop staring at Thomas as fire ants stomped drills up and down my spine.

She turned to me, confusion clear on her face. "Cassie?"

Thomas stepped in my direction, and a bolt of power shot through me, making me scramble backwards. Elliot came to me, holding my shaking limbs steady, and also stopping me from giving into the urge to run back the way we came.

"Amirel?" Thomas spoke.

I stiffened, holding out a hand as if that would keep him away from me. "Don't come anywhere near me."

Thomas's frown grew deeper. His gaze slid around our group. "What's going on?"

I held out a shaking finger in Thomas's direction. "Don't trust him."

Elliot put his hands on my shoulders. "Thomas is in our soul-group. We've known him for hundreds of years, as do Ezra and Avril. He's a Light-Stream worker, same as you and I, and Ben."

"There's something about him. I can't explain it, but we can't trust him," I said. I had no foundation for the unease that slithered up my spine, only that I couldn't get past the distrust.

"What's going on? You don't know me?" Thomas sounded unsure, his voice thick and clouded.

"I've never seen you before in my life," I said, which was true. It didn't matter that my life comprised a few short days.

Thomas gasped and Elliot stepped in. "Her mind is fracturing. Hadriel's power is too much for her. We have to perform the Heart Stone ceremony to help her. If not..."

"She doesn't remember who she is?" Ben asked, aghast.

Thomas cursed. Something like pain crossed his face before he looked at me, his eyes filled with sadness. "You're feeling the residue of my last moment on Earth. Amirel - *Cassie* - I'm so sorry. I used Leonard to get close to Walsh. He knew Lilith possessed Walsh. He helped Lilith escape to bring Hadriel out of hiding. I couldn't let her get away. Walsh is...was..." He scrubbed his hands down his face. "I wouldn't let anything stand in my way. I didn't intend to hurt you, but that is the nature of the veil."

"Except that Lilith found out about Hadriel's power and wants to kill me for it," I said.

I enjoyed seeing him wince, but my enjoyment was cut short when the stench of sulphur filled the cavern and soul-eaters surrounded us.

Elliot bundled me in his arms. Thomas, Ben, Avril and Ezra surrounded me, protecting me with their bodies. I rammed my hands over my ears, trying to muffle the soul-eaters triumphant screech.

Wind whipped my clothing and tossed my hair into my eyes as they circled us, caging us, a whirlwind of terror. Elliot hissed as a soul-eater raked its claw down his back. Ben cried out as another tore his bicep. One by one, the soul-eaters lashed out, tearing into whomever they could harm.

This was a game to them. A sick game. They were playing with us. Torturing us. Elliot cried out and jolted. Warm blood sprayed over my face as the bloom of crimson coated his shoulders. His hands trembled and he held me tight. Protecting me with his body.

"We can run, we can..." Avril cried out as her cheek opened up. Blood welled and dripped from her jaw.

But I knew they would never let us go. We were prey. They would pick off everyone one by one and then they would take me to Lilith, who would kill me for Hadriel's power.

Hadriel's power.

I was the only one who could get us out of here.

Jagged pain lanced my skull as I dug into the white stream of power deep within me. It didn't matter that my knees buckled, or the headband burned my skin, or that what I knew of myself chipped the edges of my fragmented mind, scattering them into the darkest recesses of my soul.

It didn't matter how hard I shattered because if I didn't do this, we were dead anyway.

I willed the light to bend. Willed it to annihilate the soul-eaters. To consume them the way they would consume us. Energy surged through me, exploding from my marrow and out through the centre of my forehead.

White light blinded me, filling the room, filling my vision. I trembled with the power I'd unleashed, muscles locked, blood boiling. It raced from me, too much, too hard. It poured out of me, a river of destruction that I couldn't stop, decimating the soul-eaters - but what else?

A voice hazed the edge of my consciousness. Persistent. A grip on my shoulder helped me fight the torrent.

"Cassie!" Elliot called me above the roar in my ears.

I had to pull the energy back. If not, I would hurt him. It would take him from me. I screamed, fighting to rein in the flow. I cut it off, bit by bit until the torrent became a trickle. My knees buckled. I would have fallen to the floor if powerful arms hadn't swept me off my feet.

I pried open heavy eyelids. Elliot wavered above me. His lips moved, but the white noise in my ears made it hard to hear. I tried to lift my hand to smooth the groove between his brows, but my arm was too heavy to lift.

Best I curl into his chest and sleep. Give in to the rest my body demanded. It was a sweet urge. One that was beyond temptation. That way I wouldn't have to put up with the pounding inside my skull, or the confusion that made it so hard to think. There was nothing to worry about. I could sleep for a million years if I wanted. Yes, that's exactly what I wanted.

"Don't you dare sleep, Cassie!"

My eyelids snapped open. Elliot had yelled at me? He looked angry. He barked out a command and then we were running down a dark corridor. My body bumped against his chest with each pounding step, lulling me to oblivion. Darkness. It would be so nice to curl into its soft, velvety depths and rest. Close my eyes and rest.

Someone tapped my cheek, too insistent to ignore. I groaned, swatting the hand away, but my limbs were made from the same hard stone that Elliot lay me on. Cold bit into my back, helping to push the haze away.

"Quick, Ezra, stand at the crown. Avril, you take the third eye. Thomas, the throat. Ben, stand there for the solar plexus. I'll direct the base energy," Elliot said, his voice echoing in the small chamber they'd brought me into.

The stone walls weren't a surprise, but the swirling green clouds above me were. Streams of green of all hues, from the deepest emerald to the brightest grassy green, billowed and shimmered as though lit from within. The mass coated the ceiling right above me, an unnatural substance that looked as heavy as water, yet floated as light as air, streaked with pure light and deep shadow.

"We need someone for the sacral," Ezra said.

"We have no one else. This will work. It *has* to," Elliot said, the words pouring from him in an urgent stream. "There's no time to waste. She's fracturing too much."

Semi-circular alcoves were chiselled into the rock, one at my head and feet, and one on either side of me. They moved into positions, leaving the alcove at my hips empty. As they stepped into the alive, light of all different colours lit from the ground, throwing streams of light up their bodies.

Ezra was washed in purple, Avril in indigo. Thomas was lit in light blue, while Ben was awash in yellow. Red light coated Elliot. A rainbow of colours lit them. The lights arched over their heads and merged with the green mass above me. The mass throbbed and sensation prickled within my chest.

Elliot bent to kiss me, brushing a strand of hair off my face. I blinked up at him, lost in his emerald eyes that held such weight. "This *will* work, Cassie. It will."

It has to. I heard his unspoken words, but they strangely didn't worry me. I tried to smile at him. To let him know I was fine. That I'd happily let the floaty darkness wash me away. I was happy to rest, but my lips were too thick, my tongue a slug inside my mouth, and then I looked into the green mass over my heart and lost myself in the sight. It was beautiful, with its glowing streams of light.

My eyelids were too heavy to keep open and I let them droop. The stone wasn't cold under me anymore. Nor was it uncomfortable. I was warm and relaxed.

"Now!" Elliot barked.

Their voices filled the cavern. Avril's feminine voice mixed with the deeper masculine tones. Elliot had spoken this language before. The serpentine syntaxes whispered off their tongues. Their words fluttered around me, filling me with warmth.

A name flew into my mind, momentarily anchoring in my head. Enochian. They spoke the Enochian language.

The green mass came alive with inner lights. The rainbow of colours surrounding their bodies grew brighter. They reached into the green, where they swirled and merged.

The green mass throbbed and bulged in the middle. It swelled and formed a point above me, spinning and glowing from within, until the brightest green limned the entire mass.

The colours trailed into the point and a laser beam of mixed colour shot from the point to the centre of my chest.

Heat sank through my skin, tore through my muscles, and invaded my bones. My vision white washed and then the colours lit like fireworks behind my eyes. My body became weightless and the stone underneath me dropped away. Or perhaps I rose from the stone. It didn't matter. I didn't care because reels ran through my mind, fast forwarding scene upon scene.

These weren't just scenes, or a movie.

They were my lives.

Each life began when I was born. Some ended prematurely, others lasted decades when I passed the veil as an old woman.

History unfolded before my eyes as life after life bloomed from behind my eyes. I was always surrounded by loved ones, their souls bright and sparking beneath the facade of their body. They were my soul group. We'd been each other's parents, children, cousins. Fathers. Brothers. Aunts.

Patterns of my lives became apparent. We looked after biblical objects sent to each imbued with angelic power to support the journey of humanity. Gifts bestowed on the Earth to help the growth of human souls that needed to be protected once their gift was given and absorbed into humanity.

The power was still in the objects and had to be protected, so they weren't exploited.

I saw myself die to protect these objects. I witnessed all of us find our path to becoming custodians in each life. We were Light-Stream workers. We worked with angels to accept the gifts passed through the veil, and to make sure they were used in how they were intended. Our souls made a promise. We knew our life's purpose before we incarnated. Pathways made and guided to help us on our journey.

Knowledge, experience, complete understanding were mine. The culmination of lifetimes coalesced. Fragments realigned, pieces coming together. My consciousness expanded, brushing against memories that weren't mine. Flashes of memories so distinct, so foreign, so different that they couldn't be mine skipped along the outskirts of my mind.

My soul was millennia old, but these memories were ancient. From the beginning of time when the universe exploded into life and consciousnesses were formed.

These memories were the key to the knowledge behind the power infused into the threads of my soul.

Hadriel's memories.

Memories he embedded into the power that I became.

Scattered. Disjointed. Their sharp edges latched onto mine, bringing both our minds together. Fragment after fragment fitting together, sliding into notches and valleys to lock together.

"They're coming!" Avril's urgent tone shattered my connection.

Hands grabbed my shoulders, pulling me from lying to sitting. "Cassie, we have to go.

There was more, so much more, I needed to know, to understand, but someone shook me from collecting the remaining remnants of memories, both mine and Hadriel's. Fingers dug into my shoulder, dragging me to my feet.

"Cassie! Wake up!" Elliot shouted.

My eyes were so heavy. My chest throbbed. My head pounded, my soul pulsing as though it had been cut open and was reassembled in a different pattern. But I wasn't complete. I wasn't whole.

Chakra colours swirled behind my eyes, slipping and sliding inside my body but never settling. Arms swept me up, holding me tight. My body jolted, and we were running from the cavern through a tunnel.

Howls and shrieks followed us as our footfalls pounded over stone and echoed into the darkness. I clung to Elliot, digging my fingers into his shoulders, wrapping my arms around his neck. The stench of sulphur stung my nose and clogged my arms.

"In here!" Avril said.

We darted around a corner, sliding into a large cavernous room. Shadows leapt at us. Elliot cried out as rough hands grabbed me and tore me from my soul-mate. The world spun around me as I hit the floor. My knees cracked against the stone, my palm scraped over grit before something smashed their palm on the side of my head and ground my cheek to the floor.

Triumphant shrieks cried out as they pushed me to the floor. The breath sawed in and out of my lungs. My heart thrashed behind my sternum, galloping wild and uncontrolled.

"Elliot!" I tried to speak, but I had no air. No voice. Not even a wheeze.

Bodies pressed on me, crushing me, squeezing me to the unforgiving stone.

"Don't damage her!" A shrill voice cut through the excited screeches. I sucked in a deep breath as the pressure of bodies released. Rough hands picked me up hauling me to my knees.

Lilith loomed over me, her red lips stretched into a grin.

Chapter Sixteen

"Well now, look what my beautiful creatures finally found."

Demons and half-human creatures deformed through the darkness of their souls held Elliot and the rest of my soul group in their claws.

"Let her go!" Elliot struggled against the demon holding him. The demon grinned, revealing long, thick canines, and popped its claws through Elliot's shoulder. Elliot cried out as blood oozed from the wound, staining his shirt.

Thomas's hoarse cry merged with the trills and laughter at Elliot's pain. I pulled against the hands holding me down. The half humans dug their fingers into me, squeezing bone and muscle. A cry fell past my lips as pain lashed down my arm.

"Let Walsh go, Lilith. You don't need her body anymore," Thomas said. One of the tortured pushed him to the ground and pinned him with his foot on Thomas' back.

I might still be fractured, but most of my mind was back together. Although I wasn't fully recovered, I knew enough. Thomas had incarnated to protect the artefacts. He hadn't meant to double cross us. I didn't know how General Walsh was connected, but if Thomas was protecting her, that was all I needed to know.

"Don't be so melodramatic," Lilith said, sneering at Elliot. "This will all be over in a minute, and then I'll finish off your little soul group quickly. There's no need to suffer. I have enough suffering souls to keep me entertained. Besides, I find myself impatient to get out of here. Somewhere where the stench of brimstone and guilt doesn't permeate the air."

Lilith stretched her fingers on my temples. Her lips stretched in the semblance of a smile that didn't reach the chilled deadness in her eyes, and the crystal between her breasts sparkled. "Now. Where were we?"

Lilith's energy cut into my skull, burning-cold and jagged. Ice cold raced through me as Lilith gouged her way inside me. It scoured deep inside me, into the well of power. Her energy hooked into the power, drawing it out of me with licks of icy-fire. Her energy invaded mine.

I gagged as her energy suffocated me, smothering me. I knew this energy. I'd felt it when she'd dug into me before. Ice-cold. Dark. It was familiar in a way I wished I'd never known.

Her intent became my own. It sank into me, dark, twisted and depraved. Her need for power. To control. To rend and kill and annihilate to get to her goal. She would let nothing and no one stand in her way until she ruled over it all.

She wanted to be the supreme being.

My vision tunnelled. Ropes of darkness spiralled around me. A tear ruptured deep within my chest as my soul, imbued with the power, began to flay me apart.

A light twinkled in the darkness, barely there. A silvery strand brushed against the glimmer. Our minds touched and in that split second, I'd found Walsh. Dying. Her soul was still in her body that Lilith had possessed. Her soul stuffed into the crystal around Lilth's neck, wearing her like a piece of depraved jewellery.

A memory brushed a distant part of my mind. Hadriel imbued his power into inanimate objects, hiding them, keeping them secure, locking them away with a twist of power that made it impossible to undo.

Hadriel's knowledge became mine. Lilith and I were connected. She was powerful.

But so was I.

Our souls were connected and I knew her brand of energy. In order to take the power, she had to open herself up to me.

She had let me inside her.

Thanks to Hadriel's memories, I'd found her weakness.

I slid along the silvery strands of the power as it flowed from me and let myself seep into her darkness. I dove under her energy, using it as cover until I came to the web of her essence. In the centre was a ball of inky darkness. The centre of her soul. Wisps of smoke rose off an endless inky globe at her core.

My essence bled into hers as she drained me. My heart thumped, sluggish. Elliot's scream echoed in my head, and I slumped in immovable hands. My life essence leached from me as I gathered the power that could tear through universes and fashioned it into an invisible net. I wove the threads along Lilith's essence, drawing it around the ball.

Close. I was so close, and yet I might have been a million miles away. I had to concentrate. Had to think. If I didn't...if I couldn't...

I was heavy. Light faded away. I focussed on the net, drawing it closer. Tighter. It was so hard to concentrate now. My consciousness hazed.

Tired.

I was so tired.

"Cassie!" Elliot's voice echoed in my ears, hollow and filled with pain.

I tried to listen, but Lilith was too strong. She took and took and took, and I was just...so...exhausted.

"Cassie! Fight her!"

I wanted to let him know I was trying. That I was fighting for him. For us.

Us.

I was one half of a beautiful soul.

We were joined, Elliot and I. I reached out to our connection, letting his warmth, his life, his love flow into me. Energy flowed through me, freely given. Elliot's essence poured into me. I opened up for him, letting his soul fill every crevice of mine, imbuing it with the power running through me.

I became him and he became me. We connected at a deeper level than we ever had before, the power carving into us and bringing us back together again, two halves of the one nucleus.

I used the last of my will and harnessed the ball of power around Lilith's darkness. Lilith's screech echoed in my mind. Her energy throbbed, red and painful in my grasp, and she fought against the power. I used the strength of our soul connection to keep Lilith bound. I glimpsed crimson skin, long scraggly white hair and four hands tipped with thin black claws. This was the true Lilith. The Lilith depicted in the paintings. A twisted creature who possessed bodies to be human. She screamed. The sound stabbed through my head with the force of an iron stake.

I tore along the threads of her essence towards the crystal where she'd trapped Walsh. I reached into the wall of shimmery silver, finding Walsh's soul. I yanked her out and thrust Lilith through the wall of the crystal at the same time, exchanging one for the other.

Long black claws gouged my essence filling me with molten ice as I forced Lilith through. I screamed as pain shot through every cell in my body. Thick, inky shadows bled into me so cold I would never be warm again. I ignored the pain. I had only moments to lock her in the crystal.

Angelic words flew from my lips, binding the crystal with my power, with my intent.

Lilith screamed, pounding against the wall with her strength.

But I was stronger, and unlike Lilith, I had everything to lose.

I sealed the crystal, locking it tightly with the power that could annihilate dimensions. I drew my soul threads from Walsh's body back into mine, reclaiming everything Lilith had tried to strip from me, but forever changed.

My soul wasn't just mine. Elliot and I were connected so deep that the power flowed between us, pulsing with life. With love.

The last fractures in my mind snapped together.

I.

Remembered.

I was Cassie, but I was also Lucy, Alice, Tyee, Randvoan, Ezhan and a thousand others. Names were nothing. My soul never changed. Only grew, hanging in knowledge, texture, experiences and learning, and now my growth included Hadriel's memories and power, and also opening myself to my soul-mate on a level I never knew could exist.

I looked at the demons holding Elliot and spoke through clenched teeth. They had no right to touch him. "Get your hands off him."

Of course they didn't listen. Their souls were so dark they got off on pain. On control. I called on the power flowing through me, my skin lighting up so brightly the shadows bled from the room. The demons holding Elliot flew off their three-toed feet, slammed into the stone walls, and slumped to the ground.

I shrugged my shoulders with a burst of energy, throwing off the creatures holding me on my knees. I stood, reaching for Elliot, and threaded my fingers with his. The power thrummed between us. Elliot's skin lit from within, the brightness coming from us bleeding the darkness from the room, letting me see clearly where we were.

I didn't want to think about the blood on the walls, or the fact that more emaciated bodies were chained and lost in the shadows. I could free them, but it wouldn't make any difference. The chains would reappear and they would put themselves back on the wall. The truth was, they could free themselves any time they wanted. Their chains would fall from their wrists and they could pass to the next dimension without any fight or argument. Just as the half deformed humans shaking before me could become whole and healthy in a second if they wished. It was up to them. Their shackles and their deformities were self imposed.

"Let them go." I spoke to the demons still holding Ben, Thomas, Ezra and Avril. These demons were different.

The creatures glanced at each other, their yellow eyes glowing and slitted, probably working out how they could do the most amount of damage. Unlike human souls, demons were created in the dark. Born out of human fear and guilt, they were made from anger, rage and despair.

I flicked my fingers, sending a wave of power towards them. They hit the stone, their bones crunching. The rest of the beings in the room cowered, shading their faces from the light Elliot and I threw out.

Walsh staggered, her knees buckling as she drew in a deep breath. She appeared as her physical form, her body no longer manipulated to look something else by Lilith. Thomas leapt towards her, holding her when she would have fallen to the floor, his arms banded about her shoulders and waist.

"Are you all right, Madeline?" Thomas asked.

I recognised Thomas. Everything was clear now I'd regained the fragments of my soul. Incarnated on the Earth plane as my grandson with Elliot from my last life as Marie. His original name was Ashur, and I'd known him for millennia.

Madeline leaned against Thomas, a frown on her face. She squinted, horror dawning her face when she took everything in. She clutched Thomas's hand, curling against his broad frame.

"Where am I?" she said.

Thomas turned her head into his chest, hiding her from the horrors of the room. "Lilith brought you to Hellioth. It's not a place you should even be aware of."

She curled into him willingly. Accepting his protection without a second thought. This was a new development. As was Laura's relationship with Thadius back on the Earth plane. Soul groups were made of seven souls. Elliot, Laura, Ben, Thomas, Jenny and David were a part of mine. Madeline and Thadius definitely weren't a part of our connection, but it was clear there was growth between these four souls outside of our group.

"I...I feel so weak," Madeline said.

"Your physical body shouldn't be here," I said. Lilith had used Walsh's body, bringing her here even though she would weaken and eventually die, Madeline's soul forever tied to Hellioth. Unlike the souls who brought themselves here, Madeline would never have been able to leave.

"What are you talking about?" Walsh said. She tilted her chin and straightened her shoulders, but I didn't miss the tremble that passed through them, or the way she clung to Thomas. Her gaze slid around the room, eyes wide and dark.

"It means we have to get you out of there," Thomas said.

The crystal around Madeline's neck sparkled a deep crimson. It pulsed like an artery, glittering with deep reds and vibrant scarlet. I cupped the gem, feeling it throb beneath my fingers before I tugged the chain off Walsh's neck.

Madeline gasped, her hand fluttering to her bare neck, but I hardly noticed her. My attention locked on the hypnotising throb of the gem, so like the ruby Hadriel had tattooed into my skin to escape the grey-mists. This gem could become me too. I had the power to let it absorb into my body. It had happened before, and I could do it again.

Tempting. So tempting.

I brought the crystal to my chest, right over my heart. It pulsed, warm and enticing. I shut my eyes, ready to let it sink into me.

An explosion cracked through the castle. The ground quaked beneath my feet. Blocks of rubble fell from the ceiling and a window frame collapsed, the stones crumbling to the floor. The half humans wailed and demons shrieked. A stone dropped from the ceiling, exploding on the floor. Elliot's arms came around me, keeping me on my feet as the quaking grew more violent. An ear-shattering screech blasted into the room, echoing into every crack and crevice inside. Through the crumbing window, hordes of soul-eaters filled the crimson sky and descended towards the castle, black clouds broiling behind them.

My children. Come to me.

My hand lifted as the words whispered through my mind, welcoming these creatures to be at my side. My chilled blood warmed at the sight of them.

"Open a portal, Cassie. Get us out of here," Elliot said.

I shook my head, clearing the fog and coming back to my senses. *What the hell was I doing staring at those abominations like that?*

I'd acted on urges that shouldn't be there. I'd *wanted* the soul-eaters to come to me. I'd *wanted* demons crouching at my feet. I shuddered as a frigid chill swept through my body, the urge still there, but no time to consider it.

I drew a deep breath, drawing Hadriel's — my — power. It responded to my call, flowing through me as easily as blood, as air, as life. Silvery-white light tunnelled in front of me, spinning into existence from the size of a pinprick to grow to more than my body height.

The beings in the room howled, cowering from the intense portal light. They preferred the darkness, the vibration similar to that of their souls. Anything made from light hurt them.

"Quickly, everyone through," I said.

Avril and Ezra led. Thomas took Walsh's hand and Ben followed. I gripped Elliot's hand and stepped into the light and into the courtyard of the University of Creation. The portal closed behind us, cutting off the soul-eaters shrieks and howls of demons as we stepped from the portal.

Rubble scattered across the once-perfect lawn. The roses on the bushes were wilted or dead, the grass yellowed. Behind me, the hallowed walls of the university were destroyed, chunks missing out of the perfectly manifested facade. Billowing clouds stole the sun from the sky, coating everything in semi-darkness.

Silence weighed around my shoulders, so absolute blood pounded through my ears like the beats of a bass drum. The hallways were empty. The garden bare. My stomach hollowed and rolled, squeezing with an invisible hand.

"Where is everyone?" I asked, the thought forming into words. "What the hell happened here?"

"Hello?" Elliot called. His voice echoed off the broken walls and through the crumbling hallowed hallways.

All of those souls who resided here had vanished. As though they'd simply ceased to exist.

"It can't be, but...this can't happen," Ben said, shaking his head as though he couldn't believe the desecration surrounding us.

The dimensions were indestructible, manifested from millennia of souls' growth, each dimension manifesting in a vibration to match the expansion of humanity. It was a never-ending expansion, and everlasting. Enduring through all time and space.

Or it should be.

A frown formed on Thomas's face. His shoulders set in a tense line while he still held Madeline safely in his arms. "Soul-eaters have done this."

"They didn't do this to the Hellioth dimension," I said.

"Lilith must have commanded this," Elliot said.

"She wanted to rule all dimensions. She wanted beings to worship her, so why would she destroy this?" Millions of human and non-human souls lived in each dimension. Millions of souls hunted down and cease to exist. Yet, if she killed souls, nobody could worship her. She wanted adoration. To control. It made little sense that she would kill the very thing she wanted.

Overhead, black clouds thickened, rolling towards us, billowing and expanding and pressing down on us. The crystal throbbed in my hand. A thrum of satisfaction and ice shot through me, coming from nowhere and overshadowing my terror.

Screeches shrieked in the distance, growing louder until the ear-splitting sound bounced off the wreckage surrounding us. Soul-eaters filled the sky, emerging from clouds and descending on us like a plague of locusts. Their wispy forms shadowed the sky, turning the grey light into complete darkness. Thousands of them plunged from the sky.

They'd hidden in the clouds. Thousands and thousands of them, multiplying one after the other after the other, using the dimension of creation's special qualities to manifest their own reality. No wonder Lilith had sent them here. She didn't have to create them. They had manifested themselves into an unbeatable army and now the soul-eaters were coming to finish us off.

Chapter Seventeen

Power burned the ice from my veins, humming to life along with the healthy dose of self preservation. My heart pounded against my ribs, and the breath stuck in my lungs. There were so many of them. Too many of them. I clenched my hands into fists, warring with the innate urge to turn and flee

But I couldn't do that. I had to stand and fight. I had to kill these soul-eaters. They'd done so much damage. Too much damage. There were millions of dimensions and parallel universes and there was no telling if they'd leeched elsewhere. What they'd destroyed and who they'd killed.

"Elliot, take everyone and hide," I said.

"No, we'll fight with you. You're not alone." Elliot tugged me close to him, his body thrumming with tension. Fear and determination warred with complete faith in his emerald gaze. In me.

"We're not going anywhere," Thomas said.

"By your side. Always," Ben said.

I swallowed hard. I didn't deserve that type of faith. Not the type of faith that transcended life, but then Elliot's soul brushed against mine, his essence flowing into my mind and my heart. The depth of his belief in me nearly brought me to his knees. The lingering ice in my veins didn't stand a chance as heat pulsed through me.

Soul-mates. We were soul-mates. Our souls linked, but if the soul-eaters overpowered me, they would take Elliot too.

If that happened, our soul group would splinter apart, their souls fading, unable to grow, existing without purpose. These souls were my family. My reason for living.

Elliot was my *everything*.

"You can do this, Cassie. Hadriel didn't give his power to anyone. He waited for the right person and he gave it to you," Elliot said.

Elliot's belief resounded inside me, and the power responded. It hummed to life, flowing through my body and making me tingle as I looked toward the soul-eaters rounding the top of the university.

Power burst from me as I surrounded us in a ball of silvery-white energy. The first line of soul-eaters flew down on us. The impact vibrated through my body and I surged with heat as the energy flared, surrounding them in pure white light, leaving nothing when it contracted. Not even ash. Not a sign they existed at all.

Body after body streamed towards us, pounding us through sheer force of numbers. Power flared with each impact. Tears streaked from my eyes through the intense white light of the assault. Each thunderous impact drove through my body, jackhammering my bones and jittering through my head. Each collision jarred through the stream of power, interrupting the flow, making me weaker. Sweat beaded my brow. Big fat drops ran down my spine.

"I...can't keep this up," I cried, my voice fracturing.

The power flickered. Avril cried out as claws struck through the protective shell. Madeline curled into Thomas's embrace. Darkness flickered around us and my knees wobbled. Elliot caught me with a powerful arm around my waist, and I caved against him.

"Get us out of here, Cassie," Elliot said.

I was failing him. Failing us all.

"I should be strong enough," I said, shuddering as soul-eater upon soul-eater slammed into the shell, sacrificing themselves so that another could get to us. Through sheer numbers they would.

Ice flooded my veins, weakening me, as though something inside me wanted the power to fail. Wanted the soul-eaters to consume us. My power flickered and for a moment there was nothing as darkness flooded us when my power shut off. I grit my teeth, forcing the power to reignite, breath shuddering in my throat.

"Take us somewhere safe. Somewhere to give us time," Elliot said, the line between his brows deepening in concern.

"Take us back to Earth, Amirel," Thomas said.

"Is Earth any safer?" When we'd left Earth, both soul-eaters and demons had escaped. My breath came in hard, fast pants. Earth could be overrun with soul-eaters and demons. They'd escaped as Elliot and I had stepped through the portal after Lilith.

We'd been here for weeks.

The souls there could be annihilated as they'd done here, leaving nothing but a barren wasteland. My sister. My parents in my life as Cassie - *our soul group* - only three of the billions who might have been consumed.

I gripped my stomach as unbelievable pain radiated through me. "Elliot. Siel. What if...?" I wanted to say, what if there was no one left? What if they'd already been consumed. What if there was nothing left to go back and save, but the words turned to ash on my tongue.

His jaw clenched. My pain mirrored back at me through his eyes. "We have to try."

He was right. If we lost our soul group, we had nothing. But we wouldn't know until we saw for ourselves.

The relentless flow of soul-eaters continued to ram my protective ball. Constant. Unstoppable. If we stayed, they would get us.

"Open a portal, Cassie. We have to leave." There was heartbreak in Elliot's voice. Heartbreak for the souls already taken, and for those we could not protect.

"We can get to our soul group in time. The portal can cross time and space with Earth," Thomas said.

I squinted at him through tear-filled eyes. Pain radiated through me. Each hit feeling as though the soul-eater was striking my body and not the wall of energy. I couldn't keep this up. Didn't know if I could even open a portal to save us at this point.

"That's right!" Elliot said. "Earth is a growth dimension, meaning souls can access Earth at any point in time in correlation to what they want to learn and experience. You can take us to the point in time where we stepped through the portal after Lilith."

I trembled, my legs buckling. Could I do this? Hadriel's memory sifted up through my mind. They were right. I *could* open a portal to any point in time. It was an aspect of Earth that had been designed into the dimension when it was created. Hadriel's memory gave me the knowledge to do that, but I was weak. The soul-eaters bearing down on me, taking all of my energy. I was barely holding it together protecting us.

Elliot held me against him, carding his fingers through my hair with his free hand, while he crushed me against him with the other. We fit together so perfectly, my smaller frame notched against his larger, muscular one.

He looked at me as though I'd never let him down. As though we could never be parted. His faith in me resounded through our soul-mate connection. He would be beside me, always. There was nothing I could say or do that could ever let him down. His love for me was unending and without bounds. It knew no time or restrictions. Love was the most valuable thing a soul could ever own. He knew I would always honour that. That I would do whatever it took to protect it. Protect us.

I had to access more power. I had to get us through.

I dug deep inside me, slipping through the consciousness of my mind to access the power embedded in my very being. The stench of sulphur and brimstone stung my nostrils. A river of black coated my insides, running through my veins, around my heart and encasing my soul.

Ropes of sticky blackness seized me. I struggled, fighting to free myself, but the ropes lashed around me, pulling me towards their black centre and plunging me inside before I could utter a sound.

Bitterness seeped into my mouth when I screamed. Foul darkness clogged my throat, forcing its way down into my chest and imprisoning the heart of my soul. I couldn't move, couldn't struggle, couldn't scream. My mind barely functioned as sheer terror dug its claws into me, yet it was sheer terror that drive myself to continue to fight.

I had to free myself from Lilith's trap. Had to warn Elliot. Had to fight the soul-eaters. Had to...

A strand of darkness shredded the seal I'd placed over the crystal and Lilith's soul tore free, shattering the crystal into a thousand tiny shards. I was a fool. I hadn't trapped Lilith in the gem. She'd hidden inside me, waiting to take over my power so she could command it herself.

Thought you could best me, Light-Stream worker?

Lilith's voice boomed around me, purring with sarcasm and satisfaction. The darkness pressed down on me, suffocating me, locking my consciousness in its solid grip. The ice-cold numbed my mind, making my thoughts thicken like sludge, terror squeezing me like the ooze around me.

Do you think you can trap someone like me? You've given me exactly what I want. Access to your power. Your body.

And Earth.

Lilith's chuckle resounded around me. I couldn't tell Elliot I was trapped in my body. That Lilith had possessed me and had access to untold power and the key to unlock it all with Hadriel's memories.

You have no idea how powerful that insignificant planet is, do you? No matter. You shall soon see. Together, we will be great. I will show you.

The darkness cleared. I saw Elliot frowning at me in concern, watching him through my own eyes. I opened my mouth to speak, but the ooze thickened in my mouth, plugging my nose and throat, suffocating me into silence.

I'll have none of that, Light-Stream worker. The only words your body will speak are the ones I say.

"I can do it, Elliot. Hold on to me and help me, and I'll get us all out of here." I spoke, but it wasn't me. My mouth moved, but the words weren't mine. Lilith drew power into my fingers tips and removed the band from my forehead. Power raced through my body, unleashed to its full force, thrumming with the force of a burning star.

"Cassie? Are you sure you should take that off?" Elliot said. I wanted to smooth the furrow from between his brows, but Lilith ignored it altogether. She leaned into him, clutching his shirt and simpering with glee as she threw it to the ground.

"I don't need it anymore, Elliot," she said. "I'm okay now."

No! I did need it. Put it back on. Please, Elliot. I'm breaking apart. It's too much. Too soon. If I fracture, I'll take you with me and I would never let that happen.

But I said none of those words, Lilith stopping them sliding off my tongue. Instead, Elliot's gaze softened in relief. His arm trembled around my body, but I only felt whispers of it. He kissed me. I felt only a semblance of his touch as his lips ghosted across mine.

Lilith lifted my hand, ploughing my fingers through his hair, holding him in place as she slipped her tongue into his mouth, kissing Elliot as though she were me. Elliot's tongue brushed against mine, kissing me back, holding me against him, his arms supporting her. Not me. He wasn't kissing me. He thought he was, but he was kissing Lilith, and he didn't know.

I jerked in Lilith's ooze, barely able to even do that, as the icy fingers of horror stabbed my heart.

Hmmm. I'm going to enjoy being you. Now, where was I?

Lilith willed the power forth. It surged through me, around me, for me. I pressed every ounce of will-power I had left in me into the surge of energy, taking us to the one point in time and space that we needed to go.

The power bent to Lilith's will. A portal opened into the room where Leonard had tried to kill me, where Hadriel had given his power to save us, where angels were still trapped, and where soul-eaters and demons were turned loose on the world.

Lilith took Elliot's hand and stepped through the portal, leading my soul-group, Madeline Walsh, Avril and Ezra, through with her into the chaos we'd left on Earth.

Elliot! I'm here. Help me! I tried to speak, to scream, to let Elliot know I was trapped inside my body, but Lilith only laughed at my futile attempts.

The power surged inside me as she called the soul-eaters through the portal with us, thousands of them pouring through and escaping out of the hole in the building's wall. Her army.

"Cassie, what are you doing? Close the portal now!" Elliot cried out as a soul-eater racked its claws down his arm. Blood bloomed on his arm and dripped to the floor. He fell to one knee, holding his arm.

I couldn't answer him. I couldn't utter a sound. All I could do was watch as Lilith's army swarmed in to invade Earth, using a portal I'd opened.

* * *

Continue the adventure with The Demon Cursed Series Book 5, **Demon Vanquished** today. A bigger threat came through the portal than Cassie's possessed body. Lilith returns to the world to take over the plans she started millennia ago, but old threat return more powerful and evil than ever before. Cassie and Elliot must do what no human souls have achieved in lifetimes of incarnation before times runs out for all existence.

* * *

Demon Vanquised

Lilith has possessed my body and tricked us all. She's stolen my power and invaded the Earth with her army of soul-eaters.

I've remembered my past lives. I know my purpose. Elliot and I are two halves of the one soul but I'm trapped in my own body as Lilith destroys everything the light-stream workers have incarnated to protect. She wants the power contained in biblical artefacts gifted to humanity throughout the ages from angels to become the most powerful being of all.

The angelic power coursing through my body is the only thing powerful enough to stop her, but she controls it. Angels are dying. The Earth will crumble. All souls will perish.

I must sacrifice myself to stop her, but if I cease to exist, so will Elliot.

* * *

Chapter One

Stomach clenching, lungs burning, I screamed as loud and hard as I could as Lilith stepped through the portal and back into Leonard's altar room. I writhed against the prison of my body as black slime wrapped around my limbs, binding my arms and clogging my throat where Lilith had stuffed my soul deep within my physical body. The sludge filled my lungs, my head, my *everything* until I was dripping with Lilith's darkness. Possessed and bound so powerfully that no one could hear my despair except me.

My soul was locked away in my own private hell, and Lilith was the Queen of my hell.

Watching from my eyes with no control, Lilith stood as Elliot, Thomas and Madeline were thrown to the floor through the force of the portal. Demons and soul-eaters parted around her as they streamed past. Her jubilance sickened me as it washed through my body. She loved her creations. These abominations were her soldiers and her children. Existing to do her bidding. Pawns for her evil.

A soul-eater slashed Elliot as it streaked past. Crimson bloomed on his arm, staining his shirt. He hissed, grabbing his arm and crouching close to the floor as more soul-eaters spewed from the portal and out of the hole in the wall.

Lilith whispered under her breath. Muted words above the roar and screech of soul-eaters, but ones that resounded around me. She commanded them, using the language of the angels to control. Soul-eaters circled the room, filling it. Choking me with sulphur, their darkness leeching the shimmering blue light of the portal until the room was thick with darkness.

Lilith ushered more words, and the soul-eaters flew through the hole in the wall to the world outside of Leonard's altar room. The soul-eaters blotted out any residual light in the city below the skyscraper we were in, leaving it a barren landscape of dark shadows.

Darkness as thick as the bonds holding me stained my mind. All of those innocent souls out there all around the globe were at risk of complete annihilation. None would stand a chance at survival.

Lilith chuckled in my ear. I cringed as far away from the sound. The bonds tightened harder, restricting me even more than I was. *You understand, light-stream worker, don't you? I can snuff all the work you've done over the centuries to advance human souls in an instant with a few words to my soldiers.*

She was going to annihilate humanity. She didn't care about these souls, and how valuable they were.

She was completely *insane*.

The centuries of being held prisoner in a crystal too much for her mind, although there was a distinct possibility she was always this way and the time spent in isolation in Hellioth did nothing but stoke her anger. Her need for revenge.

"Stop this, Lilith. Please. They're innocent," I said, but hope she'd listen turned to ash when she cackled. I should have known. She lacked the ability for any sort of empathy.

How does it feel to know that the Earth is my feeding ground? That those souls will exist merely for me to rule over? That beyond this Earth, there will be no more life for them? This will be my kingdom. I will give them everlasting life here, and they will bow to my will. I'm giving them nothing more than they've always wanted.

She was completely and irrevocably deranged. Earth was designed to allow souls to grow and flourish, not stagnant indefinitely. This was the perfect playground, and the light-stream workers purpose, to pave the road for souls to grow.

"They already have everlasting life," I said.

Fools. They think their existence ends with their physical bodies and I won't tell them any differently. They won't age. They'll be trapped in an immoral body in this dimension. I'll give them all they've ever wanted and in return they will worship me as they should have done centuries ago.

My stomach churned with lead weights. This isn't the way it should be. Lilith would stop the advancement of human souls just to rule over them? It went against the natural order, but that's been Lilith's game for centuries. There's a place in this universe for all souls, but for the first time I doubted if it should be that way.

Dread pooled in my gut, knowing what I must do. I caught sight of Elliot through Lilith's eyes. Sighted the physical body he would no longer have in this world, knowing I'd be responsible for him trapped back into an incorporeal body, but there was only one way I could stop Lilith and I had to act before she could do more damage.

Hadriel's power thrummed through my extremities, tingling in the far reaches of my mind. Still in touch with my soul, but for how long?

I gathered the power, hoping Lilith didn't notice how I drew it into me. While she stole most of the power, I still had Hadriel's memories. His knowledge. And I knew exactly what I had to do and how I needed to do it.

Her attention slid to me again, confusion and malevolence combined as I sent power lashing through Lilith's black ooze and out of my physical body with every last reserve I had. Electricity snapped through me, white hot and jagged before it snapped off. The shockwave of power burst from my center, rocketing outwards through bones and sinew into bricks and mortar. There was no way to know if I sent out too much or too little. Only that it was all I could do.

A boom echoed around us, shaking the building. Plaster dust showered us as the ceiling cracked overhead. I sagged in my bonds, exhaustion weighing me down. White haze fogged my consciousness as I clung to awareness. Lilith shrieked as the portal imploded out of existence. The soul-eaters circling the room escaped through the hole in the wall, leaving us in the wake of their devastation. The pale-blue light that shimmered around us vanished with the portal, leaving us in gloomy semi-darkness, lit only by the flickering firelight of the sconces still alive.

What have you done, light-stream worker? Lilith's voice resonated in my head, harsh and angry. Red hot slashes of rage lashed at me.

"Stopped. You," I gasped. Lethargy pulled at my consciousness. I gritted my teeth, struggling to stay awake. Needing to keep my wits about me.

"Cassie!" Elliot cried out.

He curled hunched on the floor. His wound no longer dripped blood but only because he was dressed in a 1940s trench coat and three piece suit, a fedora perched on his head, transformed to the state of his previous life. He was as intangible as I, trapped within the body I was born into in this world.

"Oh, Elliot." I sobbed even though Lilith would be the only person to hear me.

Bodies littered the ground, charred and decimated. Crimson coated the floor. A severed hand lay at my feet, while sightless eyes on another corpse stared into oblivion. All dead, their souls having snapped free of their bodies.

Leonard's remains lay discarded by the altar. His head was twisted at an angle, his stomach a wide open wound. Forever locked in the shock of his death, his mouth hung open. His soul would have ended up in its vibrational equivalent. The 'now' he created was a long way away. For him. Everything we'd fought against had turned for the worst.

The battle we stepped from before I opened the portal for the first time had just happened. This was my one winning act. Lilith didn't want to come back to this time. She wanted to come back months later when the soul-eaters had time to decimate the human population. She wanted them terrorized and easily controlled, and she wanted to walk in and dominate a population already subdued and beaten down.

You'll pay for what you've done, light-stream worker. The hiss of her words flayed my psyche.

Strands of black ooze lashed at me, whipping my head, arms, body. I clenched my eyes shut, protecting myself as much as I could, but it was useless. Whips of her rage cracked and gouged into me. White-hot agony lanced through me, each whip poisoned with her fury. All I could do was silently bear her wrath.

"Cassie, are you all right?" Elliot stood, his brow scrunched in that way that voiced his concern as he approached me.

I managed to raise my head to see through Lilith's eyes as the last of her lashes fell on me.

"Elliot," I wheezed, even though he wouldn't hear me.

You'll never touch him again. I'll make sure of it, Lilith hissed.

His hands stayed at his sides because he could no longer touch me. Perhaps that was a blessing because he wouldn't be touching me. He would touch Lilith, and would never know.

Ben helped Madeline to her feet. His hand stayed at her elbow while he kept her steady.

"Where are we?" she asked. Her hair was a mussed mess, her pupils blown. She was recovering quickly, but no soul should have to witness where she'd been and what she'd seen. I wondered what damage it would have caused her. Scars her soul would always bear.

"Back in Leonard's altar room," Elliot said, but Madeline gave no indication she heard him.

She couldn't even see him. To her, he was invisible.

I wanted Eliot's touch; his arms around me holding me with love, with care. And now I might never know that again. It didn't matter that I needed it. There was no way I could possibly touch him now.

Without Elliot's warmth I was hollow. An incomplete being without the other part of its soul. My eyes burned and I let my tears fall.

"Elliot. Oh god, Elliot!" I wheezed, the rest of my intangible heart shattering. I struggled, testing the bonds, but Lilith had me locked so tight again I could barely flinch.

Thomas cursed under his breath. A muscle worked at his jaw and my heart jumped. He could still see Elliot. It made sense because he was a part of our soul group. We would always see each other no matter the dimension.

"The portal's gone. We're trapped here," Thomas said.

Black clouds roiled outside, clogged thick with soul-eaters and demons swarming like flies. I'd imploded the portal. Our only connection between dimensions. And what was happening beyond Earth? The entire system could be collapsing and we would never know. Dimensions imploding, one after the other. All life — gone.

We might not be victims of Lilith's plan. This might be the only way we would live. If we stayed cut off, and with Hadriel's power, Lilith really would be queen.

If only I could open another portal, but I could barely move, let alone use the power again. I was barely able to keep my eyes open, pressed on all sides by the black ooze that locked me into place.

"And it seems I'm back in this state," Eliot said.

"Wait." Thomas moved to the altar, near Leonard's body. He picked something up from the ground, a band I recognized as the device Leonard used on Elliot to turn him corporeal. It would have fallen off him as he passed through the portal.

Elliot extended his arm towards Thomas. Thomas placed the band on my soulmate's wrist. Elliot's body snapped back to a physical state. A shadow appeared under him and his skin glowed with health and vitality, blood flowing through veins that were made from flesh and blood.

"Cassie!" His footsteps rang out in the silence of the room, hard, heavy and determined as he strode towards me.

His arm banded about my waist. Fingers firmed on the back of my head. His lips caught mine, hot and demanding.

Only he wasn't really kissing me.

My arms snaked around his waist without my permission. Lilith pressed my breasts against his chest, her thigh hiking up around his hip. She snared her fingers in his nape, clutched the lapel of his trenchcoat and shoved herself against him.

I gagged, cried out, shook in my bonds but Elliot didn't know he kissed Lilith. As long as I was trapped inside my own body, he never would.

I thrashed against Lilith's hold. With all my power, I pushed against the black ooze. "Stop it!"

Lilith chuckled and thrust her tongue into his mouth. She tilted her hips, rubbing her core against Elliot's thigh, blissed out on sensations as they began to spark and flutter.

Oh, I like this. I think I'll keep him for myself, for a while.

I choked on tears, utterly helpless to stop Elliot being used like this. Elliot pulled back, his green eyes gleaming as Lilith panted like a skank in heat in his arms, plastering her body hard against him. Elliot's brows tightened and the familiar line creased between his brows. His fingers released Lilith's hair, falling to her shoulder.

"Are you all right, Cassie?" He drew his knuckle down her cheek, a light caress that should be meant for me.

Instead, Lilith soaked it up, pushing her breasts against him. "I'm fine, because I'm here with you," I heard her say. "I'm just shaken up from coming back here and seeing all this carnage." She moved towards him to kiss him again.

Elliot's gaze flowed over Lilith's face. He took Lilith's hand, and squeezed it. "We'll get through this together."

"That's not me. I'm in here! Please, Elliot. Please hear me." I sobbed at the slight tilt of his head when his gaze shot behind me.

"Watch out!" Elliot leapt towards a shadow as it shot from the corner of the room towards the altar, where Dee's journal lay open.

Lilith whispered under her breath, and a soul-eater snatched the journal, darting to the hole in the outside wall. Elliot ran into its path and jumped at the soul-eater, grabbing the journal from its claws before rolling to the ground out of its way.

Sibilant words fell between Lilith's lips and the soul-eater spun on Elliot.

"No!" I screamed

The soul-eater raised its clawed hand, slashing at Elliot. His coat shredded and lines of crimson bloomed on his stomach. Elliot scrambled backwards, uttering angelic words as the soul-eater attacked.

The creature stopped. Elliot came up on his knee, his words growing louder and stronger, while Lilith continued to whisper, fighting against him. With everything I had left in me, I wrapped my fingers around the bonds at my wrists and jerked.

Lilith stuttered. Elliot came to his feet, ordering the soul-eater to go. It shrieked, a sound like nails down a chalkboard. Madeline clapped her hands over her ears, her face scrunched, while Thomas put his arms around her, hugging her to him. The soul-eater flew from the room to join the horde filling the sky outside.

Elliot staggered and winced. He put his hand across his stomach, doubling over.

That's another thing you'll pay for, light-stream worker, Lilith hissed.

"Do what you will. I'll never give up," I rasped. How I'd do that, I didn't know. Only that I would never stop fighting her.

"Elliot. Are you okay?" I cringed at the insincerity of Lilith's voice as she walked towards my soul-mate. She wouldn't know the first thing about caring.

"A creature like that would never know what this is." Elliot clutched the journal, the line a deep V between his brows.

"Then why did it try to steal it?" Thomas said.

Elliot shook his head. "I don't know, but we can't leave the journal here. We'll take it back to the Sanctum. We know it'll be safe there."

"It's the safest place on Earth," Thomas said.

Lilith hissed, the sound rattling over me.

"You'll never win against us," I said.

Little fool. Getting into your Sanctum is the place I want to be. Just think of the goodies I can use there.

My chest shrunk. The Sanctum held the most powerful objects of the Earth, put there for safekeeping against creatures like Lilith. I struggled against the black ropes but it did no good. My legs gave out. My shoulders groaned as they took the weight of my body. I needed to keep my strength. I had to fight the only way I could. Lilith had possessed me, but we weren't connected.

She'd stuffed my soul into a tiny prison inside my own body, but it took effort and concentration to keep me here. I could use these bonds against her, but only if I had the strength. I would need to bide my time. Make her think she'd beaten me down. Weakened me.

I'd do what I could to keep everyone safe and hope that Elliot would see the lie.

"We need to go back to Jenny, David, Laura and Thadius first. They're going to be worried," Thomas said.

"Agreed," Elliot said. "Careful what you say around them though." He gave Thomas and Madeline Walsh a heavy look. "They won't remember their soul journey. If we tell them too much too soon, we risk them not believing us and we'll lose them."

The doors to the altar room slammed open. Elliot wrenched my body to the ground as a gunshot boomed in the room.

"Cover. Now!" Elliot yelled.

He grabbed my arm and hauled me behind the altar as Thomas and Walsh dove for cover behind the rubble.

"Get them!" One of the thugs yelled as half a dozen men ran through the open doors, filing out along the wall to cover us. The low light didn't make their guns any less menacing. They held them with a sure, firm grip. They were men experienced in using them. Professionals.

Leonard's thugs had come to take us down.

One click Demon Vanquished today...

* * *

Want to know why Jenny tries so hard to stop Cassie from seeing ghosts? Start the adventure with The Demon Cursed Series Prequel, **Shadow Awakened** today.

Click here and join my 10 part email sequence to find out what dark happenings in Jenny's past made her try everything she could so stop the gift manifesting in her precious children.

* * *

Shadow Awakened

I'd planned on leading a quiet life as a librarian but instead I'm fired from my job, and haunted by an evil ghost who leaves me for dead and diagnosed crazy. The only kindness I receive is from a doctor in my new home, Victoria Mental Institution.

For the moment, I'm safe, but I know that won't last.

It never does.

The ghost still stalks me. He wants to destroy me and there are demons cheering him on. The only way out is to fight—aided by the inmates of the asylum.

The dead won't know won't hit them.

Fans of Laura Thalassa's 'Four Horsemen', I.T. Lucas 'Children of the Gods', and K. F. Breene 'Demigods' will devour this paranormal romance filled with angels, demons and impossible odds.

Shadow Awakened is the prequel for the Demon Cursed series. If you like strong heroines that fight for the truth, lost souls that sacrifice all and the answer to the afterlife itself, dive into this exciting series today!

* * *

Scan the QR code to be directed to start reading **Shadow Awakened** today.

Want to hear about my next release but don't want to sign up to my email list?

Follow me on BookBub
Follow me at charmainerossauthor.com